A Note to Readers

While the Allerton, Lankford, and Farley families are fictional, the events that took place in Cincinnati during 1828-29 are all too true. Many white people in the city thought that too many black people were settling in Cincinnati, so they looked for ways to drive the black people out. Other white people argued that black people had a right to live in the city.

In August 1829, between two and three hundred white men attacked "Little Africa," the black section of the city. They injured black people, destroyed property, and burned homes. After the riots, many white people became more sympathetic toward the black people and wanted to allow them to stay in the city.

Still, more than half the black people living in Cincinnati fled to Canada. They were helped by donations from Quakers and from people in New York and Pennsylvania. But much of the money used to help them resettle in Canada came from the black people who decided to continue living in Cincinnati. More than thirty years of danger to blacks and the white people who helped them passed before the beginning of the Civil War.

ESCAPE
from
SLAVERY

Norma Jean Lutz

CHELSEA HOUSE PUBLISHERS
Philadelphia

First published in hardback edition © 2000 by Chelsea House Publishers, a division of Main Line Book Co. Printed and bound in the United States of America.

© MCMXCVII by Barbour & Company, Inc. Original paperback edition published by Barbour Publishing Inc.

The Chelsea House World Wide Web address is http//www.chelseahouse.com

1 2 3 4 5 6 7 8 9 10

Library of Congress Cataloging-in-Publication Data

Lutz, Norma Jean.
  Escape from slavery / by Norma Jean Lutz ; [inside illustrations by Adam Wallenta].
      p. cm.
  Previously published : Uhrichsville, Ohio : Barbour Pub., c1997. (The American adventure ; #16)
  Summary: In nineteenth-century Cincinnati, fourteen-year-old Tim Allerton finds his anti-slavery views tested when he and his younger sister Pam save the life of a slave baby whose mother has recently been murdered.
  ISBN 0-7910-5590-6
  [1. Slavery Fiction. 2. Cincinnati (Ohio)—History Fiction. 3. Afro-Americans Fiction. 4. Christian life Fiction.] I. Wallenta, Adam, ill. II. Title. III. Series: American adventure (Uhrichsville, Ohio) ; #16.
  PZ7.L97955Es   1999
  [Fic]—dc21   99-38687
                                                                    CIP

Chapter 1
Black Laws

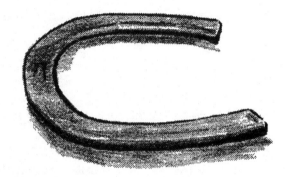

"Timothy!" came Pamela's voice from the stairway. "Mama says it's time for you to leave."

Tim Allerton didn't even lift his head from where he was bent over his work at the rolltop desk. His quill scratched furiously as he hurried to write out the last few notes. That very morning, he'd found yet another new fact in the law book that lay open before him.

All Mama wanted was for him to run a few errands. Surely there was no hurry. He turned the page in the book, dipped the quill into the ink holder, and wrote yet another line.

He'd promised to return the book to Ward Baker that day, and he meant to keep that promise. Ward, a black attorney who lived in the "Little Africa" section of Cincinnati, was kind enough to loan his books. Tim never wanted to take advantage of that generosity.

Given all the difficult subjects Tim was studying at Danenhower Private School, for which his father paid dearly, there was so little time left to study law. But law fascinated him more than all the subjects he took at school.

The sudden swishing of skirts outside his door warned him that Pamela was near. Quickly, he closed the book and slipped it into a drawer. He pulled out his Latin textbook, then shuffled the papers and put a blank sheet on top, just as her soft tap sounded on his bedroom door.

"Timothy?"

"I hear you, Pam."

"May I come in?"

"If you must." He dipped the quill again and pretended to be copying from the text.

The door opened, and his younger sister came sweeping into the room, bringing her beaming smile with her. Though she was only twelve, Pamela's loveliness commanded floods of compliments wherever she went, and not even Timothy could deny that she was pretty. In a year or so, her suitors would be legion.

Lifting the skirt of her pale green dress, she approached his desk. "I told Mama you would be studying. What a waste of a lovely Saturday morning."

Toying with one of the sausage curls that framed her face, she said, "I swear, Timothy Allerton, at fourteen you study more than most of the young men at Cincinnati College."

"Most of the young men at Cincinnati College don't have any goals except to complete their courses and get out."

Her laughing green eyes grew serious for a moment.

"What an unfair charge. How can you know the dreams of others?"

"I said 'most.' It's true of most people in Cincinnati. They're content to sit by and let things happen."

"And you would solve the problems of the world."

Tim methodically wiped his pen and sprinkled the paper with blotting sand. "I believe I can solve a few."

Pamela wrinkled her freckled nose. "Oh Timothy, you're so deep and serious." She put her hand on his shoulder in motherly fashion. "I fear you're going to grow old before you've had time to have fun being young."

Tim looked up at her and smiled. "If you keep worrying about me, you'll have wrinkles in your pretty brow before your thirteenth birthday."

Touching her forehead, she said, "Not me. Not an early wrinkle here. I know how to enjoy life." With that she stepped back and deftly executed a few dance steps, making her copper-colored curls bounce.

"The dance master who comes to Sybil's house says I have the lightest step he's ever seen." She whirled around, then stopped. "He also says I have the lightest heart."

"Stuff and nonsense." Tim pushed the papers back and pulled down the top of the rolltop desk. "What does a dance master know about your heart? He can't see your heart. Only God knows what's in a person's heart."

"There you go again. So serious. So literal."

Tim wished there were some way he could get his sister out of his room. He needed to put the law book in the back of his trousers before putting on his coat. He tried to keep the borrowed books hidden from Papa and Mama as much as possible.

"Mama says if you don't get started running errands,

7

you'll never get finished."

"But I have the entire day."

"Not if you spend the best half of it with your nose in a book."

Tim waved his hand, losing patience with his carefree sister. "Go tell her I'll be down in a moment." He stood from his chair and stretched his long legs. "See here?" Striding over to the bed, he picked up his black riding boots. "I'm getting my boots on right now."

Pamela moved to the door. "I'll tell her. May I help you saddle Fearnaught?"

"Don't you have dance steps to practice?" he asked.

"Timothy, if I didn't know you better, I'd think you were teasing me."

Tim grinned at his sister. He sat down on the chair at his desk and pulled on the shiny high-top boots. "Of course you can help."

"Oh, thank you." She gave another whirl and sped out the door.

Once she was gone, Tim got the law book out from the desk drawer and fastened it securely in the waist of his already-tight trousers. While it made breathing a little difficult, it would have to do until he got out of the house. This must be how Mama's cinched corset feels, he thought as he pulled on his frock coat and went downstairs.

Mama was in the drawing room seated at her mahogany secretary writing something. Making her list for him, no doubt. Her dark hair was looped into braids in back, and the sausage curls that framed her face were similar to Pam's. Mother and daughter spent long hours with the curling tongs to make their hair curl just so. Tim was more than thankful he didn't have to put up with such a waste of time and energy.

8

"There you are, Tim," Mama said without looking up. "Whatever took you so long?"

The sound of Tim's boots was muffled by the soft Turkish rug beneath his feet as he stepped to where she was sitting. "Mama, it's barely ten," he protested.

His mother's desk was situated in a tiny alcove next to the fireplace. The matching alcove on the opposite side held bookshelves. In the top of the arch of each alcove hung baskets of Swedish ivy that his mother and Willa, their domestic, fussed over constantly.

The drawing room, set about with heavy walnut tables, tufted cherrywood chairs, and two heavy settees, was his mother's favorite room. The colors and styles of fabric for the heavy pleated drapes had been carefully chosen by his mother. The small fire in the fireplace chased off the chill of the late October day.

"This is a far cry," he'd heard Mama say so often, "from our little cabin next to Deer Creek."

Indeed it was. The steamboat business had been good for the entire family. So good, in fact, that now Tim's father felt it was the only business to be in. Timothy strongly disagreed.

His mother blotted the paper. "I had one more thing to add," she said, folding the paper and handing it to him. "I'd nearly forgotten. The broken clasp on my brooch is being repaired at Bodley's Jewelers. I imagine it's ready by now."

Timothy gave a little groan at the mention of the Bodley name.

"Why, Tim. What's the matter?" Mama asked.

"Didn't you know, Mama," Pamela said, choosing that moment to enter the room. "Tim doesn't care much for the Bodley family."

His sister was right. Ebenezer Bodley, a vocal city council

9

member, was vehemently pro-slavery. Tim hated to be near the man. That feeling also went for his son, Hollis Bodley, who happened to be in Tim's class at school.

Mama stood and placed her hands on Timothy's shoulders. She stretched up on tiptoes to plant a light kiss on his cheek. "It does little good to dislike those who are of a different opinion, Timothy. You should know that. Mr. Bodley has a right to his opinion, just as you have a right to yours.

"Now," she continued as though the matter were settled, "Papa also wants you stop by Miller's to see how near our carriage is to being finished. He said if it's ready, the two of you could take the team by and bring it home this evening."

Tim was beginning to squirm. He also needed to stop at the blacksmith's because one of Fearnaught's shoes had come loose. With all these stops, he wasn't sure he'd have time to return Ward's book, which, still stuck in his waistband, was making breathing more and more difficult.

After returning his mother's kiss, he turned to leave with Pamela on his heels. "Remember to be polite to Mr. Bodley," Mama called after him.

Tim strode toward the kitchen where the gray-haired Willa was bustling about. "Good morning, young Tim," she called out cheerily.

"Morning," Tim said without a pause in step. As he opened the back door that led to the Allerton stables, he heard Willa say to Pamela, "What's gotten into the young master?"

"I have no idea," Pamela answered.

It was unthinkable to Tim that his own mother could approve of the likes of Ebenezer Bodley. Or worse, that she would command Tim to pay respect to the man. Such people deserved no respect.

Pamela hurried to catch up to Tim and walk beside him.

He held the stable door open to let her inside. They were met with the odor of hay mixed with sweat. Horses nickered their greetings. Papa was rightfully proud of his stable.

Quietly Pam worked with Tim to saddle Fearnaught. He knew she loved the roan Kentucky thoroughbred almost as much as he did. As Tim readied himself to mount his horse, Pam reached out to give him a pat on the back. Her hand brushed against the hard cover of his hidden book.

"My gracious, Tim. What is that in your waistband?"

"Nothing."

"Don't tell me you're borrowing books from Ward Baker again."

"If you won't ask, I won't tell." Tim pulled out the book and slipped it into the bag that hung by his saddle, thankful to take a deep breath of air again.

"Oh, Tim. Papa has asked you not to spend so much time in Little Africa. It's so dangerous."

"There you go again," he said, reaching out to touch her freckled nose. "I'm the serious one, remember. You just stay with your dance lessons, and I'll take care of my own business." He swung up into the saddle and walked Fearnaught out of the stables.

A definite chill hung in the air as he rode out of their property on Seventh Street and headed Fearnaught toward the downtown area. Only two months into the school year, Tim found he must spend every spare minute studying in order to keep up. Hollis Bodley, on the other hand, completed his assignments with ease, made high marks, and then gloated about it.

Tim's close friend Isaac Proctor, a handsome young fellow who took nothing seriously, couldn't understand why good

11

marks were so important to Tim. Ironically, Isaac's father, who owned a large, successful soap factory, wanted Isaac to attend Yale, where his older brother James now attended. Isaac chafed under the pressure to follow in his brother's footsteps.

Isaac's advice to Tim, which echoed Pamela's, was to stop taking life so seriously. Only Ward seemed to understand Tim's dreams for the future.

As Tim reined in at Carver's Blacksmith Shop and dismounted, he forced himself to put troublesome thoughts out of his mind. The sharp ring of metal hitting metal filled the air as Mr. Carver worked at his anvil. Several other men stood about talking. Seeing Tim, Mr. Carver laid down his hammer and came over. "Good day, Timothy. What can I do for you?"

"Loose shoe." Timothy gently lifted Fearnaught's right foreleg. "Can you get to it now? I'm in a bit of a hurry."

"You younguns are always in a hurry." The blacksmith wiped his hands down his leather apron. He had arms like fence posts and a reputation of knocking heads together at the drop of a hat. Tim would never want to cross him.

Mr. Carver reached up to take Fearnaught's reins. "Come on, fella. Let's see what we can do about that uncomfortable shoe."

Tim followed the blacksmith past the hot forge to the back, where he tied the horse. As Tim watched Mr. Carver work to secure the loose shoe, he could overhear bits of conversation from out front.

"Why have laws on the books if we ain't gonna enforce 'em?" The man's words were garbled from speaking through a chaw of tobacco. "That's what Councilman Bodley says. And I agree."

"I agree as well," put in another. "If the law says the blacks should put up the bond money and register, then why ain't they doin' it? If we have to abide by our laws, why don't they have to abide by theirs?"

Tim stroked Fearnaught's silken nose as he glanced toward where the men stood together in a little knot. He recognized one as a man named Sparks. The two others, better dressed than Sparks, were strangers to him.

"If they can't follow the law," the taller of the two strangers remarked sternly, "they should be told to leave. If they don't leave, they all should be run out of town."

"Councilman Bodley told me that's exactly what he's pushing for," Sparks replied. He spit a dark stream of tobacco juice off to the side. "Exactly what he's pushing for."

Tim hadn't heard much about the law they were discussing. He wondered if such laws applied to Ward and Clara and their little boy, Joseph. Why would anyone want to run a kind, gentle man like Ward Baker out of Cincinnati?

CHAPTER 2

Attorney Ward Baker

Fearnaught's hooves beat out a steady clip-clop as Timothy guided him down Fourth Street. The wide, brick-paved street was alive with traffic. Carts and wagons filled with crates and barrels competed with stately carriages.

A stagecoach full of passengers, drawn by a team of six horses, flew around the corner. Two ladies in bonnets and long shawls were forced to scurry out of the way. Tim heard the driver yell "Whoa!" as he pulled the team to a stop at the ticket office near Main Street.

Although Bodley's Jewelers was located nearby, Tim turned and rode north to the Miller's Carriage Manufactory. Saving the worst till last didn't solve anything, he knew. But there was something almost fearsome about Ebenezer Bodley. Though Tim hated to admit it, he was frightened of a man with so much power.

Geoffrey Miller manufactured fine-crafted carriages, many of which were shipped by steamboat down the Mississippi to wealthy plantation owners in the South. Outside the five-story building sat a long row of shiny new black carriages waiting for delivery. Tim tied Fearnaught to the hitching rail and stepped inside the building. It smelled of fresh-cut wood and tanned leather.

Gray-haired Mr. Miller, always friendly and congenial, led Tim into his office, away from the noise and dust. Riffling through a stack of papers, he said, "Yes, here we are. The men are putting the finishing touches on the Allerton carriage now. It should be ready to pick up this evening."

"Papa and I will bring the team by to take it home," Tim said.

"I'll have the bill of lading prepared and ready."

Tim tipped his cap and made his exit. Mounting Fearnaught, he decided he'd better return the book to Ward next. He turned his horse toward the west and headed for the street called Western Row, which led south toward Little Africa.

Many of the houses where the black folk lived were nondescript wooden dwellings. Some were crudely made shacks. A few nicer frame houses stood out from all the rest. One of these belonged to Ward Baker. Tim knew that if Ward had stayed back in New England, he could have had a highly successful law practice. But Ward felt called to be in Cincinnati. He felt that his people needed him. And he was right. While Tim admired the stand Ward had taken, such courage baffled him.

15

Recalling the harsh comments he'd heard in the black-smith's shop, it crossed his mind to hide his horse in back of the Baker home. Who knew what might happen to him or his family if someone like Hollis Bodley found out about Tim's trips to Little Africa? The very thought made him know he possessed very little of Ward's kind of courage.

At the sound of Tim's knock, slender Clara opened the door, greeting him with a warm smile. "I thought I heard you ride up. Come on in here, Timothy. How good to see you again. My, you're lookin' fine."

"Thank you, Clara. Is Ward here?"

She nodded. "In his study as usual." Spying the book in his hands, she said, "Returning another book, I see."

"Yes, ma'am. Does he have time to see me?"

Chuckling, Clara smoothed the print apron that covered her simple floor-length muslin dress. Her sleeves were pushed up as though she'd been working in the kitchen. "I dare say. Ward Baker seems to always have time for you, young man. And if little Joseph weren't taking his nap, he'd be joyous to see you as well."

Tim felt himself blushing a bit. The toddler did seem excited at his visits, jumping about and shouting, "Timo-ty, Timo-ty." Tim was sorry the tyke was asleep.

"Wait here," Clara told him, waving toward the parlor. "I'll tell Ward it's you."

Tim moved from the hallway into the parlor. It contained sturdy, yet simple furniture. Most of what Ward and Clara owned had been brought with them from Massachusetts. Since arriving in Cincinnati, Ward had earned barely enough to live on, certainly not enough to purchase any new furniture. The black folk he represented and defended had little or no money with which to pay Ward.

16

Over the fireplace hung a portrait of a black man whom Tim knew to be Ward's father, Adam. Adam's father, Cloman, whose African name had been Boto, had been captured from his village in Africa and brought over as a slave.

After several years, Cloman's master had freed the slave. Cloman then moved to New England, where he learned how to read and write. By working hard and saving his money, he saw to it that his children were well educated. He died before Ward was grown, but Ward had learned many stories about his grandfather and the people who had lived in Africa.

Tim's thoughts were interrupted by Clara's return. "Ward wants to see you in his study," she said.

"Thank you, Clara," Tim said, remembering his manners. He strode down the dim hallway to the back room that served as Ward's law office. After tapping on the door, he heard Ward answer, "Come in, Tim."

The tall black man stood up from his desk when Tim entered. He reached out a large hand to give Tim a firm handshake. "Welcome, young friend. Please come in and have a chair." Ward had a gentle face with high cheekbones and a strong, square chin. His ready smile and kind eyes always put Tim immediately at ease.

Ward waved toward the door. "Oh, and let's close the door."

Tim did as Ward asked, then took the comfortable tufted chair beside the desk. "I've come to return the book, and I thank you kindly for loaning it."

Tim loved being in Ward's office. There were shelves of books, sheaves of papers, and always work strewn about the wide cherrywood desk. One day Tim would have an office like this, and he, too, would give his services to those who were unable to help themselves.

Ward took the book without giving it a glance. "I suppose you've heard what's afoot in the city."

"The move to enforce the black laws?"

Ward nodded, his dark eyes serious.

"What does it all mean?" Tim asked. "Why now? Aren't all blacks free here?"

Ward ran his hand over his black wiry hair. Touches of gray showed at the temples. "There are white people in this city who feel the growing population of black people is dangerous. They want to stop that growth and get many of us to move out of the city."

"How do they plan to do that?"

"The city council has appointed a committee to come up with ideas. I think they will begin with the so-called black laws."

"That's what I heard some men talking about in the blacksmith's shop," Tim said. "What are these laws?"

Ward stood, stepped over to his bookshelves, and pulled down a book. "Let's have a look."

Settling his long frame back at the desk, he riffled through the pages until he found what he was looking for. "Here," he said, handing the volume to Tim.

Scanning the page, Tim caught his breath. "Why this says that any black person who settles here must have a certificate of freedom." Tim shook his head. Everyone in Cincinnati knew there were runaway slaves among the two thousand blacks in Little Africa. Those runaways would never have such a certificate.

"Read on," Ward said.

"And they're required to post a bond of five hundred dollars and enroll the name of a bondsman." Tim looked up from the page. "But that's impossible. No one in Little

18

Africa has that kind of money."

"But that's the point, Tim. If they set impossible require-
ments, we black people will have to move on."

Tim read the final requirement, forbidding blacks from
testifying in court against whites. Tim knew that part of the
law was often used when runaway slaves were brought to
court. They weren't allowed to testify about the beatings and
other cruel things white people had done to them.

"Why was such a law made in the first place?" Tim
asked.

"Fear," Ward answered. "These laws were passed back in
1804. The men in office at the time felt they could use the
laws to keep blacks under control. Then other men came into
office who saw no need for such strong measures, so the
laws were ignored."

"But now?"

"People are uneasy. I've felt it for a number of months.
Many of the men who are now in power agree with these
laws and want to see them enforced."

"I heard Ebenezer Bodley's name mentioned."

Ward nodded. "He's certainly one of the more vocal
ones, and he seems to have swayed several council members
over to his way of thinking."

"He has wealth on his side," Tim said, thinking of the
lavish jewelry store on Fourth Street.

"Money often turns the hearts of good men."

Tim closed the book and handed it back to Ward. "Does
Clara know?"

"We don't talk about it much, but she feels it, too. She
suggested we pack up and move to Canada while everything's quiet."

Tim held his breath. "What did you tell her?"

19

"It's not the Lord's timing just yet. There's still work for us to do here."

"I admire your courage, Ward. I'm not sure I could do the same if I were you."

Ward rested his hand on Tim's shoulder. "Never forget, my friend. Courage is not the absence of fear. It's merely walking into the face of fear."

Tim nodded, but he still wasn't fully convinced. "I must be going," he said as he stood.

"Thank you for listening, Timothy. Because you plan to study law, you should be aware of what's happening. Now then," Ward said, as he stood and scanned his bookshelf, "what would be good for you to read next? Oh, yes. Here. A book that James Madison wrote before helping to draft the Constitution."

Tim took the volume and thanked Ward.

"Can you stay for tea? Clara would love to have you. And I believe I hear young Joseph bouncing about." Ward opened the door of the office and led Timothy down the hallway.

"Thank you, but I must go. I've yet another errand to run before returning home."

"Another time, perhaps. A time when I am not doing all the talking."

Joseph, barely two, came toddling toward Tim and grabbed his legs with squeals of joy. Tim placed the book on a table, then lifted up the bright-eyed child and swung him to the ceiling, making him giggle.

"He adores you, Tim," Clara said. "How good it is for him to see a white person. . ."

"Now, Clara," Ward interrupted. "There are plenty of good-hearted white folk out there."

20

"Yes, of course. But we don't see many of them in our parlor, now do we?" she said as Tim handed Joseph back into her arms.

Tim grabbed his book and made his departure, thanking Ward once again. As he rode back up Western Row, Tim remembered the day he'd first met Ward in the Cincinnati public library. Tim had been surveying the small section of law books. He'd read nearly everything the library had to offer. Ward wanted to know what a boy so young was doing reading law books.

After learning of Tim's desire to study law, Ward immediately befriended him and offered the loan of his books. Though Papa never forbade Tim from going to see Ward, Tim knew his father didn't much like the idea. How he wished he and his father could see eye to eye on more issues.

Traffic on Fourth and Vine had picked up since earlier that morning. Tim guided Fearnaught in and out among the wagons, drays, and carriages, tipping his cap to people he knew.

Bodley's Jewelers was located in the center of the block on Fourth between the hatter and the hardware store. Tim tried to remember what Ward had said about walking into the face of fear. Perhaps he wouldn't even see Ebenezer Bodley or his son, Hollis. Tying Fearnaught's reins to the hitching post, Tim strode inside.

He seldom had reason to visit the shop, and he'd almost forgotten how opulent the interior was. Ornate gilt carvings adorned the arched ceilings, from which hung the newest gas chandeliers. Tim had heard from his school friends that the crystal chandeliers came from Paris.

Long rows of cases lined each side of the room. Well-dressed, courteous clerks stood at attention. The store was bustling with Cincinnati's wealthiest citizens—men with top hats and canes, and ladies in poke bonnets and ruffled shawls. Tim felt awkward and out of place.

He shifted from one foot to the other, wondering what he should do next. Suddenly a voice sounded from behind him. "Well, if it isn't the Allerton boy."

Tim turned and looked straight at Ebenezer Bodley. The close-set beady eyes and narrow, pointed face reminded Tim of a weasel. Mr. Bodley's pale delicate hands were clasped together. He bounced upon his toes as he said, "Now, young man, what can we do for you?"

"My mama, that is, Mrs. Richard Allerton, left her brooch here to have the clasp repaired. I've come to pick it up."

"I see." Scanning the store, Ebenezer spied his son. "Since you're a school chum of Hollis's, I'll let him wait on you." Raising his voice just a bit, he called out for his son and motioned for him to come.

Tim saw Hollis pause and measure the situation before putting down what was in his hands and walking toward them.

"Hollis, look here. One of your schoolmates. His mother left a brooch here to be repaired. See about it, will you?"

Hollis had many of his father's features: slender build, a pinched face, and the same beady eyes that narrowed as he studied Tim.

"Well, don't just stand there," Mr. Bodley said stiffly.

"Yes, sir," Hollis answered. "Follow me," he said to Tim.

Tim followed Hollis through the crowded store, past all the glass cases, to the back where the repairs were made. Several customers were clustered about, also waiting for clerks to assist them.

"Allerton, Allerton," Hollis said as he went through the

list of names. The numbers beside the names evidently corresponded with the packages on the shelf. "Ah yes, Allerton. Here we are."

He turned to take a small box off the shelf. "Allerton of the Lankford and Allerton Boatworks. The family with the stable full of the finest horses in Cincinnati."

Hollis turned back around and put the box and its bill on the counter in front of Tim. Gazing at Tim with his dark beady eyes, he added so everyone nearby could hear, "One of which, a fine roan, I believe, can be seen periodically going in and out of Little Africa."

All conversation stopped. Tim felt the eyes of customers and clerks alike staring at him.

CHAPTER 3

Tim Takes a Stand

Tim's mouth went dry and his palms grew clammy. How could Hollis know about Tim's visits to Little Africa? Saying a quick prayer, Tim took the box and opened it to look at the new clasp on Mama's brooch.

"Fine work," he said. Reaching into the pocket of his waistcoat, he pulled out the coins to pay for the repair. "My papa always told me that only old ladies and little girls gossip." Tim tucked the small box into his pocket and turned to go. Then he added, "Do you suppose my papa was wrong?"

A few chuckles sounded from customers standing nearby as they turned back to their business. Hollis's face turned a shade whiter.

Satisfied with the effect of his words, Tim strode through the store and back outside. As he rode off, his insides felt like a mass of quivering jelly. He was sure to have to deal with Hollis's anger at school next week.

Later that evening, Tim and Papa took Papa's matched team to Miller's Carriage Manufactory. Tim followed along on Fearnaught, and Papa rode bareback astride one of the team horses. Mr. Miller had the carriage waiting out front. As they hitched the team to the brand new enclosed carriage, Tim could see the pride glowing on his father's face. He watched as Papa paid Mr. Miller the full amount for the carriage.

Ever since Papa had begun working with Paul and George Lankford at the boatworks, the family income had seen a marked increase. Many wealthy owners of river packets preferred to have their new boats built by the Lankford and Allerton team. And that success had moved the Allertons from their cabin on the outskirts of town to one of the fine, large homes on Seventh Street.

Papa suggested Tim tie Fearnaught behind the carriage and ride up on the carriage with him. Tim liked being on his horse much better, but he didn't want to refuse Papa's invitation.

Behind their large home, Papa had had a spacious carriage house built directly beside the stables. A small open carriage was already parked inside. It was here that they brought the new family carriage.

When they pulled up behind the house, Mama, Pamela, and Uncle Ben came out of the house to cheer the new arrival. Tim wasn't sure what all the fuss was about. After all, it was just a carriage. Even Willa stepped out of the kitchen, wiping her hands on her apron and sporting a wide grin.

Mama waited for Papa to step down and open the door for her to look inside. "Oh, Richard," Tim heard her say, "it's lovely enough for a queen."

"And you're my queen, Susannah," Papa answered as he gave her a hand up.

"Then that makes me a princess," Pamela quipped. She peered inside where Mama was now sitting. "Gracious! It is lovely. I don't believe I've ever seen such a splendid carriage in all Cincinnati." Papa gave her a hand up, and she settled in beside Mama.

Uncle Ben, Papa's younger brother who lived with the family, ran his hand over the smooth lacquered finish. "Expert woodworking," he commented. Uncle Ben loved working with wood and did much of the ornate woodwork that went into the steamboats. Very soon he would be opening his own furniture factory just up the street from the public landing.

"May we all take a ride, Papa?" Pamela asked, hardly able to contain her excitement.

"Not a one of you'll be riding now," Willa spoke up. "Dinner's ready and waiting. I'll not have the gravy getting lumpy and my sponge cake falling."

Mama laughed. "Willa's right. We can all take a ride soon enough. Ben, you help Richard unhitch the team while Tim takes care of Fearnaught." Taking Papa's hand, Mama stepped down. "By the time you come inside and wash, dinner will be on the table."

Later, as the family was seated in the dining room enjoying another of Willa's scrumptious meals, Tim mulled over the events of the day, paying scant attention to the conversation whirling about him.

Pamela was asking Uncle Ben how he was doing on Emma's cedar dowry chest. Emma Schiller, a German girl,

26

was Uncle Ben's betrothed, and he talked of little else but Emma and their upcoming wedding. Uncle Ben spent a great deal of time in the German district of the city. The girl's family hadn't much money, so Uncle Ben had offered to make the chest for her.

Uncle Ben replied that the cedar chest was nearly finished and that they were trying to decide where they would set up housekeeping.

Tim thought it all quite boring. Emma Schiller was nice enough, but she was such a plain girl. Not at all the type of person Tim thought Uncle Ben would take for a wife. When Tim was younger, he'd looked up to his uncle, thinking that Ben Allerton could do anything. Now, much as Tim hated to admit it, he was somewhat disappointed in his uncle. And in Papa, as well.

Conversation turned to Uncle Ben's new furniture factory and the details of how it would work. Papa advised Uncle Ben to begin his business by manufacturing furniture specifically for the Lankford and Allerton steamboats.

"That way," Papa said, "we can help you get a good start. After all, why should we contract for furniture from Louisville or Pittsburgh when we can buy it from you right up the street?"

"I appreciate your help, Richard," Uncle Ben answered, "but what I really want to do is create exclusive pieces of fine furniture."

"And you will, of course," Papa assured him. "But it's best to start small and work up. Why, I remember when Paul and George and I built one or two boats a year. Look how we've grown from that."

Papa cut another large slice of ham and passed the platter to Mama. "Now we're in a position to help Tim here get started. He won't have to struggle like we did."

"I know Tim appreciates that," Mama said.

Only then did Tim realize his name had been mentioned. "What?" he said looking up.

"Paul and George and I have been discussing the best place for you to start out," Papa went on. "We'd prefer for you to learn all facets of the business. That way you'll be in the best position to take over someday."

Tim squirmed in his chair. "Papa," he said softly, "we've talked about this before. I want to study law, not the steamboat business."

"There are too many attorneys," Papa said with a wave of his fork. "You can always study law on the side. In fact, Cincinnati College will be offering night classes soon. Nothing wrong with studying law if you have good business knowledge to fall back on."

If Tim had told his father once, he'd told him a dozen times about his longing to attend Harvard. But Papa continued to act as though Tim had never said anything about going to Boston for college.

"Besides," Papa continued, "at fourteen, you can't be certain what you want. Give it a few years, and then you'll know. Meanwhile, we'll be needing your help all next summer. We're counting on you, Son."

Pamela, trying to be kind, shifted the focus of conversation to the Society of St. Cecilia. The entire family knew that for several months she'd been longing to be invited into the group. "I didn't even think I'd be eligible," she said, "but Sybil O'Bannon is putting in a good word for me."

Sybil's father owned the largest mill on the landing, and Tim knew they were one of the wealthier families in the entire city.

"I think that's splendid, dear," Mama put in. She seemed relieved to turn to a safer subject. "When will you know if you've been accepted?"

"Sybil said I'd be told before the holidays. If I'm accepted, I'll be included in the holiday festivities. Perhaps even a dance."

"A dance?" Uncle Ben exclaimed. "You're not even thirteen. That's too young for a dance."

"Oh, Uncle Ben," Pamela said with a laugh. "Are you becoming old fashioned at twenty-two? Of course we have dances. Why Sybil's been studying under her dance master for over a year. It's great fun and a perfect way to make new friends."

Tim couldn't imagine his sister having time for more friends. She seemed to have dozens as it was. While he and Isaac Proctor were pretty good friends, Tim didn't hit it off with most of the other boys at Danenhower School. The nearest person he had to being a true friend was Ward Baker.

Just then, Uncle Ben mentioned that he'd heard talk of the city council bringing up the black laws. "I hear some folks asking why have laws if we're not going to enforce them. Others are saying these weren't good laws to begin with and should be repealed. From what I can tell, tempers are hot on both sides."

"The council must have a good reason for bringing it up again," Papa said.

Tim spoke up. "Enforcing such a law would be the same as driving all the blacks from their homes. It would be cruel and inhumane." His words surprised even him. His ears grew hot as Papa studied him.

"Tim, have you been listening to the black folk talking?" When Tim didn't answer, Papa continued. "Remember

29

which direction Cincinnati faces? Do you?"

"South, sir."

"That's right. We face South, and the business of our city depends on trade with the South. That's why it's important for us to keep our noses out of such things and remain neutral. Same way with the slavery issue. If the Southerners want to hold slaves, that's their business and none of ours. We can't tell them how to live."

Tim wanted to remind his father that he'd not remained neutral when he'd escaped from the British as a young man. But Tim knew he had already said enough.

"Do we have an understanding?" Papa asked, looking straight at Tim.

"Yes, sir."

"Neutrality is the key," Papa concluded. "Neutrality is the wisest course."

"Yes, sir," Tim repeated. But he knew in his heart he could never be neutral. In his heart he'd already taken a stand.

CHAPTER 4

Stage Fright

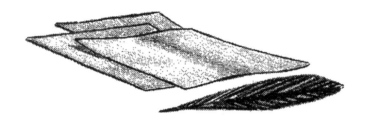

Timothy wasn't sure how his problems with Hollis Bodley first developed. The previous year, Tim had barely noticed the skinny boy. Tim's main concern was to study hard and keep his grades up. As a result, he'd finished the spring term with the highest marks in the class. Except in elocution, that is. He'd always been afraid of speaking in front of a group.

Over the summer, Hollis had experienced a growth spurt. Though he was still thin, he had acquired a swagger and a cocky attitude. From the first day of school, he made it clear he was determined to knock Tim out of the position of best student in the class.

Tim's friend Isaac Proctor told him to ignore Hollis. "He

toots his own horn," Isaac said. "And rather loudly I might add."

At first, it was easy to take Isaac's advice. Hollis Bodley was no more than a minor irritation. But then Hollis became bent on making everyone aware of the situation, which embarrassed Tim to no end.

On the Monday following Tim's visit to the jewelry store, their instructor, Mr. Rohmer, called the two of them to the blackboard to work calculus problems. Hollis said loudly, "Smarty pants Mr. Allerton only thinks he's the smartest student in Danenhower School. Just watch this."

Though Mr. Rohmer shushed him, Hollis had turned a simple class exercise into a contest. What was worse, the class members loved it. Tim's palms grew damp, and his stomach tightened. When the problem was given, he found his mind spinning. Hollis finished first, and when he did, the class cheered.

Tim was dumbfounded. It shouldn't have mattered who finished first, but Hollis had made it matter. When Tim sat down, he felt hot and flushed. Hollis had bested him by just a few boastful words.

Later, during elocution, Tim planned to give a recitation of a speech by James Madison. Madison had been president during the War of 1812, and Tim highly admired him. Presenting a speech was enough to give him heart failure, but because of the episode with Hollis that morning, he was even more nervous.

Sure enough, while he tried to present his speech, Hollis passed notes, whispered, and created little signs that he held up for those behind him to see. Tim was amazed that Mr. Rohmer paid no mind to the twittering and snickers. At one point Tim completely forgot the lines and had to be prompted by Mr. Rohmer.

By the time he bungled through to the end of the speech and took his seat, Tim was fuming. Hollis might stand a few inches taller, but Tim was sure he could trounce him good. All he needed was to get his hands on him. Right after school, perhaps. Just outside the schoolyard.

Isaac caught Tim's eye from a few rows over and rolled his eyes. At least Isaac seemed to understand his frustration. Tim was disappointed that Mr. Rohmer hadn't taken care of the problem.

Their white-haired teacher with his full bushy sideburns was soft-spoken, yet a stern disciplinarian. His dark eyes snapped when he was angry. So why hadn't he cracked down on Hollis?

Other speakers followed Tim, but Hollis tormented none of them. That made Tim even angrier.

Just before school let out for the day, Mr. Rohmer announced that he was going to set up four debate teams. "Elocution isn't enough in and of itself," he told them. "You must learn to think on your feet and to reason and deduct clearly. Debate will achieve these goals for each of you."

By having the students count off, he divided them into four groups. To Tim's surprise, Mr. Rohmer included the girls. By luck, Isaac was on the same team as Tim, and there were only two girls.

"Take a moment now and elect your captains," Mr. Rohmer told them. "Then announce to the class your first idea for a debate subject."

The teams left their desks and met in clusters off to the sides of the room.

"Well," Isaac said to Tim with a grin. "You're the one who wants to be the attorney. I move Timothy Allerton be our captain."

Isaac looked around the group for any opposition. Finding none, he said, "All in favor, raise your right hand." It was unanimous. Tim felt like he'd been set up.

"You have about fifteen minutes remaining," Mr. Rohmer announced from the front of the room. "Time to decide on your subjects."

"Timothy, here," Isaac informed the group, "has strong feelings against slavery. So I feel we should debate something about the issues of slavery."

Tim saw the disturbed looks on the faces in the group. "Naw, Isaac," he countered. "That's too controversial for the classroom. No need riling up hostile feelings for a measly school assignment."

"I agree," said a girl named Priscilla. "A much more important issue, and one that affects us right here in the city, is the problem of cows and pigs in the streets. My papa says it should be outlawed. The filth and stench is a detriment to the city. Not to mention what a nuisance they are. And who could forget that poor child who was mangled by pigs a few years ago?"

Tim winced inwardly. Animal-free streets could never be more important than the issue of slavery, but he let the remark pass.

"Isaac, fetch paper to write our resolve," Tim said.

From his desk, Isaac brought his quill and a sheet of clean paper. Dipping the quill in the inkwell of the desk nearest them, he wrote as Priscilla dictated.

"Resolved," she said, "inasmuch as cows and pigs. . ."

"Stray livestock," Tim put in. "Covers more area."

"Inasmuch," she began again, "as stray livestock create filth and stench in our city streets, citizens should keep all livestock fenced for the betterment of the health and well-being of others."

34

Tim was surprised at her clear reasoning. Isaac read it back and then looked at Tim. Tim nodded. The others agreed. It was a good debate subject. After all, city hall had been arguing about it for several years.

Within minutes, Mr. Rohmer directed them to return to their seats. "Each team captain will stand and read their debate resolution to the class," he said.

Tim went first. When he read their subject, Hollis snickered. Tim heard him whisper, "Ooh. Such a strong forthright subject."

When Hollis stood up as captain of his team, Tim could hardly believe it. Why would anyone vote for him as a leader? Then Hollis read their resolution: "Resolved: inasmuch as the area of Little Africa poses a threat to the entire community with shoddy housing, filth, disease, and high rates of criminal acts, the black laws that are already on the books should be immediately and strongly enforced."

Tim felt as though he'd been kicked in the stomach.

Luckily for Hollis Bodley, Mr. Rohmer asked Tim to remain after class for a moment. Otherwise, Tim wasn't sure what he might have done.

After the classroom was empty, Tim approached the platform where Mr. Rohmer sat at his desk. For a few moments the elderly instructor riffled through a few papers as though Tim weren't there. Then he looked up and said, "I suppose you're wondering why I didn't put a stop to Hollis's shenanigans today."

Tim swallowed around the tightness in his throat. "I did wonder that, sir."

Mr. Rohmer raked at his bushy sideburns. "I understand you want to be an attorney. Is that correct?"

"That's correct, sir."

"Ever been in a courtroom?"

Tim had gone once with Ward. "Yes, sir."

Mr. Rohmer looked up at Tim. His eyes were kind and gentle. "The courtroom is a wild and wooly place. Sometimes ruthless."

The man paused, and Tim waited patiently to see what he was getting at. "I don't know what kind of burr Hollis has under his saddle," he continued, "but I have a hunch."

"Could you tell me, sir?"

Shaking his head, Mr. Rohmer said, "Not now. We'll let things take their course for a time. You've heard me say this a number of times, Timothy, but I'll say it again. I want my students to learn to learn and to learn to think. If I tell you life's answers, then I've failed to do that. Is that clear?"

"I think so, sir."

"The elements of a formal debate present an excellent arena of practice for you, Timothy, in many ways."

"You didn't set this up just for me. . ."

The old man chuckled. "No, of course not. But it can be for you if you think of it that way."

"Do you feel I hedged today?"

"What I feel or don't feel isn't important."

Tim didn't answer. He kept thinking about Ward. What would Ward have done in this situation? He wouldn't have backed down from the issues when so much was at stake.

"You may go now, young man. I hope I've given you something to think about."

"You have, sir. Thank you."

As he left the room and walked down the hall to the stairway, Tim was filled with new resolve. He still wasn't sure why Hollis was so determined to show him up, but he knew one thing. He needed to keep a clear, cool head and not let his anger fly out of control.

Tim increased his pace, knowing that Pamela would be wondering about him. Pushing open the heavy front door of Danenhower School, he expected his sister to be right there waiting for him. No one was about. Surely she wouldn't have gone on home without him.

Tim hurried down the front steps. Then he saw them. Near the front wrought iron gate stood Pamela, lost in deep conversation with Hollis. She was leaning with her back against the fence, her long ruffled shawl fluttering in the cool afternoon breeze. Her pretty face, framed by a stylish poke bonnet, gazed up at Hollis with avid interest.

Timothy exploded. Running toward them, he yelled out, "Hollis Bodley, you get away from my sister!"

CHAPTER 5

New Courage

Tim would never forget the look of surprise and hurt in Pamela's eyes as she saw him coming toward her. Or the smirk on Hollis's face.

Hollis never moved an inch. "I believe," he said calmly, "that your sister is plenty old enough to choose her own company."

Never had Tim wanted to hurt someone as much as he wanted to hurt Hollis at that moment. Struggling to contain his anger, he put his arm about Pam's shoulder and guided her through the gate.

"Come on," he said. "We're late."

It would have been easier for Tim if Pamela had given him a good tongue-lashing, but gentle-natured Pam never did such things. Tim knew he'd embarrassed her, and he ached inside because of it.

They walked along in uncomfortable silence until finally Pamela said, "Hollis was only being polite. He said it wasn't proper for a girl to stand outside alone. He said, 'Especially such a pretty girl.' He was very nice."

Tim's jaws were clenched.

"I'm sorry if I made you angry," she said softly.

"I wasn't angry at you," he managed to say.

"At Hollis, then? He's such a nice boy. Why are you angry with him?"

Tim stopped and turned to his sister. "Pamela, Hollis's father is a councilman."

"I know that," she said.

"And he's one of those men who are trying to enforce the black laws. The laws are unfair and would place an incredible hardship on the black community in our city."

Pam's eyes were wide, but uncomprehending. "What does that have to do with me?"

"Hollis agrees with his father."

"Are you saying we shouldn't speak to those with whom we may disagree?"

Now that Tim thought about it, he wasn't sure what he was saying. How would he ever be an effective attorney if he couldn't clarify his own thoughts?

"Oh, never mind," he said sharply and started walking again. His stride lengthened. Pamela lifted her skirt to hurry after him.

When they reached the house, Tim headed for the stables.

"Aren't you coming in to greet Mama?"

"Tell Mama I'll be back later. I've something I must do," Tim said, ignoring the troubled look in Pam's eyes.

Quickly he saddled Fearnaught and rode across town to

Ward's house. Only Ward would understand.

Once he and Ward were alone in the attorney's study, Tim poured out the events of the day. He even explained how Isaac had suggested the slavery issue and Tim had backed down.

"I was afraid, Ward. That's the simple truth of it." It felt good to get it all off his chest. "How will I be of any use to anyone if I'm afraid?"

Before Ward could answer, Tim described the scene outside the school with Hollis. "Not only did I give in to fear, but I gave in to anger as well. I made a fool of myself and embarrassed my sister. I don't know how you do it. You face danger almost daily."

At that point, Clara tapped on the door and brought in a tray with tea and cake. When she was gone, Ward handed a cup to Tim and said, "I don't know that any of us become truly free of fear."

"But you never. . ."

"Never what? Shake and tremble? Give in? You just don't know, young Timothy, what goes on inside of a man. Remember what I told you about courage not being the absence of fear? When you take a stand for what is right, the Lord supplies the grace to help you through the dark times."

"If I give Him a chance. Is that it?"

"If you give Him a chance," Ward repeated.

Tim then reported what Mr. Rohmer had said after school.

"He sounds like a fine instructor. You are fortunate to have him. To learn to think is a priceless quality. It's what men do without thinking that they later regret." Ward helped himself to a second piece of cake. "So, what are you going to do?"

Tim sipped the hot tea, grateful for the momentary distraction. Though he should have been hungry, he didn't feel like eating cake. "I was hoping you might tell me what to do."

"You take the first step."

Tim thought a moment. "I'd like to meet with my debate

team and try to persuade them to change the resolution. I want to tackle the issue of slavery itself."

"Good beginning."

Tim looked at Ward, then brightened. "Why, I could get details from you. About your grandfather, Cloman, and the stories he told you of how he was kidnapped from his village and put into chains."

"Go on."

Tim's mind was racing with ideas. "And there are probably others in Little Africa who could tell stories of the horrors of slavery."

Ward was smiling now. "And what about presentation?"

"Oh, yes. There's my awful fear of speaking in front of people. I don't know what to do about that."

"Maybe that's where I can help. How about if I teach you? There are a few tricks that can help you concentrate and relax."

"Tricks?"

"Of course. Attorneys and politicians use them all the time."

Suddenly the cake looked quite appetizing. Tim picked up the plate and fork and took a big bite. "Tricks for relaxing. Now that would be just what the doctor ordered."

Ward pulled out his pocket watch. "It's getting close to your suppertime. Before you come back next time, list the points you feel would be most effective in your presentation. We'll discuss them, and perhaps I can help you strengthen each point."

Finishing the cake, Tim stood to go. "Thank you, Ward. I feel much better now."

"This may turn out to be a blessing, Tim. Thank the Lord for Hollis Bodley. His kind can teach you how to walk in God's grace. And once you learn the lesson well, no one can take that knowledge from you."

As Ward opened the office door, he added, "One more

thing. Keep in mind that you cannot force Pamela to agree with you. Be patient. Pray for God to give her eyes to see truth."

Tim nodded. "I'll try to do that. And thanks again."

As he rode home, Tim was filled with excitement. Whatever Ward told him to do, he'd work hard to do it. It would be worth it just to finally overcome his fear of speaking in front of a group.

The matter of Pamela wouldn't be quite so easy. He felt Hollis had talked with his sister that afternoon just to get Tim angry. The memory of the two of them standing by the fence still made him fume. But Ward was right. Tim would have to pray for patience.

Tim arrived at school early the next morning, armed with a sheet of prepared notes. Before school began, he gathered his debate team and apologized for backing down when the slavery issue had been mentioned. Isaac had a twinkle in his eye as he listened intently.

It wasn't easy to change the minds of his group. "Abolishing slavery would ruin the South," a boy named Lander Wilson argued. "No one wants to see that happen."

Isaac replied with a grin, "Don't get so serious, Lander. Our little school debate won't ruin the South. All we're doing is introducing a subject for a school project, not submitting an amendment to the Constitution."

Priscilla still felt they should focus on the problems of livestock in the streets. Tim answered that perhaps they could address that subject in another debate. After some thought, she finally agreed. They took a vote, and it was done. Their debate would be about the abolition of slavery.

CHAPTER 6

The Lyceum

"Attention, class," Mr. Rohmer said after he'd taken the roll. "One of our debate teams has an announcement to make. They've changed their subject. Timothy, as the captain, would you inform the class of that change?"

Though Tim was nervous, he also felt a surge of excitement. He knew he'd made the right decision. "Yes, sir," he said, taking his paper and standing before the class.

Not bothering to give Hollis a glance, he began to read. "Resolved: inasmuch as the Declaration of Independence deems that all men are created equal and that the Creator God gave certain unalienable rights, among which are life, liberty, and the pursuit of happiness, and inasmuch as all blacks are human beings created by God, and inasmuch as the institution of slavery destroys families and brings personal agony and grief to all those bound by it, slavery in the United States of America should be abolished."

The class was quiet. No one dared breathe. Only then did Tim glance at Hollis. His eyes were hot with anger. Isaac, however, gave Tim a smile of encouragement.

Breaking into the silence, Mr. Rohmer asked Tim to be seated. He announced that the actual debates would begin in three weeks. "I will allow time in the afternoons for you to work on your arguments. In a few days we'll draw straws to see which teams compete against each other.

"As a good preparation for your debates," he went on, "I suggest you attend the lectures and debates at the lyceum as often as possible. As the future leading citizens of this community, it would behoove you to keep abreast of all that's going on in the world. Reading the newspapers and going to the lyceum are the best ways to do that." Waving to a broadside posted on the wall, he added, "Please note the times and schedules of upcoming speakers."

Tim wasn't so sure that newspapers always printed the truth. He wished Mr. Rohmer had mentioned the pamphlets and brochures printed by the abolitionist groups. Tim sent for such materials as often as he could and found that they were much more reliable than the opinions of Cincinnati editors.

When the teams met that afternoon to work on their arguments, Tim was pleased with how his team worked together. Whether each member believed the resolution wasn't important, they all wanted to win the debate and were willing to throw themselves into preparing to do a good job.

When the bell sounded the end of class, Lander suggested they stay a few minutes longer in order to finish the point they were discussing. Mr. Rohmer was agreeable. When Isaac and Tim finally walked out the front door, there was a repeat of the previous day. At the gate, Hollis stood talking with Pamela. Again, Tim felt anger exploding inside him.

"Easy now, Tim," Isaac warned.

"I told him yesterday to stay away from her," Tim said as he clenched and unclenched his fists.

"He wants you to do something like punch him. Think how sorry Pamela would feel for the bloke then."

Tim knew Isaac was right. And Pam would never forgive him if he displayed his anger right there on the school grounds. He took a deep breath as they approached the pair. Pam looked his way with questions in her eyes.

"Afternoon, Miss Pamela," Isaac called out, tipping his cap. "Nice to see you."

"Thank you, Isaac," Pamela replied. "Nice to see you, too."

"You can be plenty proud of your brother today." Isaac walked right up and stepped between Hollis and Pamela, forcing Hollis to step back.

"Is that so?" Pamela said. "Truth be known, Isaac, I'm proud of my brother every day."

Isaac turned to Tim. "Now see there, Timothy. Wasn't I just commenting about how close the two of you are? It's a freak of nature, that's what it is."

As he talked, he maneuvered around to force Hollis to move a couple more steps back. "Why, my older sister would never say such nice things about me. And my brother says even less."

"One can easily see why," Hollis quipped in a nasty tone.

"What was that?" Isaac glanced over his shoulder. "Oh, it's you, Hollis. Why, yes, you're right, one can see why. You talk as though you know my elder siblings. They are quite taken with themselves."

"You were saying about Tim?" Pamela prompted.

"Yes, well, your brother is captain of our debate team."

"You are, Tim?" Pam's green eyes brightened. "You never told me that."

Hollis attempted to step around Isaac and said, "I'm head of one of the other teams."

"And that's not the half," Isaac said, moving directly in front of Hollis once again.

"Please do tell the other half," Pam insisted.

"He was courageous enough to re-state our resolution and take a stand for abolition."

Pam glanced at Tim, then over Isaac's shoulder at Hollis.

"Miss Pamela doesn't agree with the abolitionist movement," Hollis said in an acid tone.

Tim looked at Pam, but she was quiet. Finally she replied, "I only said that I dislike violence and that I believe we should show mercy to those who own slaves. Who are we to judge another's way? The Scriptures are clear in that area."

Tim felt himself stiffen. "We also learn from the Scriptures that we are to hate that which is evil."

"But if the owners love their slaves, is it truly evil?" Pamela asked.

"Seldom do they love their slaves," Tim countered.

Hollis stepped up once again. "Is this the closeness you referred to, Isaac?" he asked with a wicked grin.

"We need to be getting home," Tim said curtly.

"Good day, Miss Pamela. I so enjoyed our conversation before it was rudely interrupted." Hollis stepped up to take Pamela's hand as though he were a gentleman taking his lady to the theater. What was worse, she allowed him to do so.

Isaac shrugged his shoulders and spread his hands as if to say to Tim that he'd done all he could to help.

"Good day, Hollis," Pamela said, giving a little curtsy.

Timothy turned to go. He couldn't bear to watch.

"Tim," Isaac called out. "We're still going to the lyceum tomorrow evening, right?"

Not looking back, Tim waved his hand. "Yes, we'll go." After he'd gone a few steps, Pamela hurried to catch up to him.

"It would be most polite of you to wait for me."

Tim didn't answer.

"You're angry with me again, aren't you?"

"I can't believe you're so blind that you can't see you're putting fuel on the fire inside of Hollis."

"And what of the fire that burns inside of you, I'd like to know," she retorted. "Hollis is a kind, polite young man, and I see no reason to hurt his feelings. While you and he may disagree, I see none of the anger in him that I see in you."

Her words cut deeply. How could Tim explain to her that his anger was against injustice? He couldn't stand the suffering that Ward and Clara and all of their people went through every day. How could he explain to Pam the fear that people in Little Africa lived with daily?

In Pam's protected world, such fear didn't exist. Tim longed for his sister's understanding, but for now, he knew it was not to be.

The next evening, lines formed outside the lyceum nearly an hour before the doors opened. Timothy and Isaac arrived early to get the best seats.

"I suppose one day it'll be you up on that stage," Isaac quipped as they made their way into the large auditorium.

"I must conquer my stage fright first."

"Now for me, I'd just like to have a string of fine racing horses, Kentucky bred of course, and let father's soap factory take care of me."

Tim gave his friend a sidelong glance to see if he were joking. Of course he was. Isaac was seldom serious about anything.

"If only it weren't for James," Isaac said, referring to his older brother. "We received notice recently that he's at the top of his class at Yale." Isaac led the way into the third row, then slouched down in his seat, rumpling his expensive frock coat. "Do you know how worthless that makes me appear?"

"You're no dimwit, Isaac. With just a bit of effort you would do far better than me in every class."

"Oh, and now you want to speak like my father." Isaac lowered his voice a bit as the seats filled in around them. "Believe me, Tim, nothing I could do would ever top James's accomplishments." He shrugged. "I learned a long time ago it's just not worth the effort."

"But isn't there something you want apart from being who James is?"

Isaac chuckled. "Yes, Tim, there is. To be apart from James!"

Tim laughed at the joke in spite of himself.

"And now Naomi makes it even worse," Isaac said, referring to his older sister. "She's married a well-to-do Easterner, so I'm compared to my brother-in-law as well." He shook his head. "I've been shot down before I've even spread my wings."

Tim understood Isaac's dilemma in some ways. After all, Tim's father believed that he should follow the other men of the family and become involved in the boatworks. But he didn't fit there, no more than Isaac would fit in at Yale.

When the formal lecture finally began, Tim pulled a small pencil and notepad from the pocket of his waistcoat. He planned to take notes, not only of the subject, but also of how the speaker conducted himself in front of an audience. He noticed the man's use of his voice, the meaningful pauses, and the eye contact. Surely he could learn to do that.

Later into the program, Tim leaned over to Isaac and whispered, "Even if you aren't excelling at Danenhower as your father wishes, will you at least help us win the debate?"

Isaac laughed softly. "If only to silence a puffed-up peacock by the name of Hollis Bodley, I pledge to do my utmost to cause us to win."

Tim nodded. He knew he could count on Isaac.

CHAPTER 7

The Debate

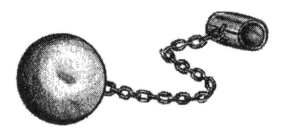

True to his word, Ward not only instructed Tim in speaking techniques, he also taught him ways to strengthen his arguments. Tim learned more details about the story of Ward's grandfather, Cloman, being taken from his village and family.

"Grandpa never forgot the day members of an enemy tribe attacked his village and captured him. They put him in chains, marched him across the rugged African terrain, and sold him to some white men who lived on the coast," Ward told him. "He was kept in a pen until a ship arrived. He spoke of the horror of the slave house. It was some sort of stone structure into which the captured men were taken, some screaming and fighting."

As usual, they were sitting in Ward's study. Tim was transfixed, appalled that such things could actually happen. He'd had his pencil out to write, but he found it difficult to write while listening to such terrifying stories.

"They were led down a long corridor of the building, then roughly pushed through an opening, falling into the ships below. My grandfather was fortunate enough to be put on a 'loose' ship. At least he could sit up and move about."

Ward was pacing back and forth in his small office as he spoke. "He later learned that other black men came over on ships that practiced 'tight' packing. The slaves were packed, lying down, so tightly into the holds of the ship that they were unable to move. Many died on the way.

"Don't forget to add in your talk," Ward continued, "that the law against slave trade was passed by our legislature in 1807. Twenty-two years ago. No one enforces it." Ward shook his head sadly. "All that law accomplished was to increase the illegal smuggling of slaves."

As Tim and Ward continued to work on the debate, Ward would often give Tim a speech to read and then distract him. One time he had Clara go outside and tap on the window to try to break Tim's concentration. Slowly, Tim learned to ignore any distraction.

Each afternoon at school, as Tim worked with his team, he sensed that they, too, were appalled at the details they were learning. Priscilla grew teary-eyed at the account of the kidnapping of Cloman. "Why, I never thought of these folks having families over there in Africa," she said.

Each member of the team helped plan the order in which they'd present their arguments. As the days passed, Tim began to look forward to the actual debate, even though he

51

wondered how Hollis was planning on trying to disrupt the presentation.

Early in November, Pamela learned she'd been accepted into the Society of St. Cecilia. After that, Tim heard nothing but talk about the society. Either Sybil O'Bannon was at the Allerton house or Pam was at the O'Bannon home almost every day. Both were anticipating being inducted into the society during the holidays.

As fall gradually gave way to the cold days of winter, Tim spent even more hours in his upstairs room studying. His grades had to excel if he ever expected to be accepted into Harvard. And he did expect to go to Harvard, no matter what plans his father might have for him.

The drawing for the debates did not turn out as Tim had hoped. He wanted his team to present the rebuttal to Hollis's argument on the Cincinnati black laws. Instead, one of the other teams drew that position. Their rebuttal, he told Isaac, was weaker than a paper roof in a hailstorm. Hollis's team won hands down.

Tim's team then presented rebuttals to a resolution that tax funds be allocated to build a substantial bridge across the Ohio River. Although Tim believed that a bridge would benefit everyone, with Ward's help, he was able to put forth a convincing argument that the huge cost of such a project would never be worth the effort. His team won by a narrow margin.

When it came time for Tim's team to present their argument for abolition, Hollis's group drew the longer straw. This meant the final debate just before Christmas would be between their two teams. Tim groaned inwardly when he found out. But Isaac appeared delighted.

When Tim reported this turn of events to Ward, he admitted how nervous he was becoming. "Much as I would like to defeat Hollis, I still wish we'd drawn one of the other teams," Tim told Ward. "Hollis can be ruthless."

"What better place to prove yourself?" Ward asked. "Remember what I've taught you. You're not thinking of simply winning a debate. You have a chance to educate those around you. You have the advantage of using compassion in your presentation. The other team only has arguments about money to fall back on."

Tim knew Ward was right. This was the chance for him to present much of the abolitionist information printed in the pamphlets he'd been reading.

"Who knows," Ward said, "you may change the mind of one of your classmates. Years from now, that one boy may become tomorrow's leading citizen, speaking out against slavery."

Tim liked that thought. It would help him get through this nerve-wracking assignment. Mr. Rohmer had told them that the results of the debate would make up a large percentage of their grade in elocution.

That evening, when Tim arrived home from Ward's house, he found Mother and Pamela busily decking the house in garlands and festive decorations.

"Tim, there you are," Pamela called out as he came in the back door. "Would you kindly help us?" She was twisting greenery around the balustrade of the staircase that came into the back hall. Mama was standing back, cocking her head to see if the garlands were hung correctly.

Tim politely greeted Mama with a kiss on her cheek. As he hung his long cloak in the closet beneath the stairs, he said, "You know the debate is tomorrow afternoon, Pam.

Much as I'd like to help, I still have last-minute notes to assemble."

"Oh, Tim," Pam lamented, "it's nearly Christmas. Why can't you break free and have fun for a change?"

"Perhaps after the debate is over. For now, Ward says I must remain undistracted."

"Is this the debate that's made your father so unhappy?" Mama asked.

Tim knew his choice of subject matter had been unsettling to his family, but he never thought of it making Father unhappy.

"It's only a school activity," Tim said. "One I must do in order to receive passing marks."

"We certainly don't want you to forego making good marks," Mama said, "but I see no reason for you to have chosen such a heated subject for your debate."

"It's a subject I strongly believe in," Tim replied. "Because I believe in it, I'll be more persuasive. Hopefully, that will gain me the high marks that I need."

Mama just shook her head. Seeing she didn't understand, he shrugged and turned toward the stairs. "I'll be in my room until supper," he told them.

"You're upstairs until supper every night," Pam complained. "And then after supper as well. Sybil and her mother are coming to call this evening. Won't you please come down and be civil to our company?"

Tim was halfway up the stairs. "They're coming to see you, not me."

When he reached the top step, he heard Pamela call out, "They'd be here to see you if you were somewhere to be seen."

During supper, Mother happened to mention Tim's

upcoming debate. Tim wished she hadn't, for it gave Father the opportunity to express his displeasure once more.

"I've tried to make you understand that remaining neutral is the policy this family will take in these matters," Papa stated solemnly. "Yet you choose to go against my wishes."

"It's a school assignment," Tim repeated, but he had to admit to himself that the debate had become more than a simple assignment. It was an important mission. Thankfully, the remainder of the dinner conversation consisted of Mama and Pamela chatting about upcoming holiday activities.

Later that evening, Tim heard Pamela calling upstairs, asking that he come down and greet their guests. On the rolltop desk before him lay sheets of paper where he had meticulously copied all his notes so every team member would have a copy. There were still two more copies to go before he finished. He had no desire to see Mrs. O'Bannon or her daughter.

In a few minutes, however, giggles and swishing skirts sounded outside his door. "Timothy," came Pamela's voice as she gave a light knock. "May we come in?"

Tim heaved a sigh. Why couldn't he be left alone? "Come in if you feel you must."

In a moment his room was filled with two giggling girls who had nothing of any importance to say. Tim tried to mask his impatience at this interruption as Pamela politely presented Sybil. Tim greeted her as civilly as he could, hoping the visit would be short.

"I understand you're preparing notes for the big debate tomorrow," Sybil commented. She waved her hand at the untidy stack of papers.

"Pamela told you?" Tim said.

"Of course Pam has spoken of it, but it's the talk of the

entire school as well."

Tim looked at her with surprise. It had never occurred to him that the debates affected any of the other classes. "It is?"

Sybil, seemingly pleased to have caught his interest, went on. "Possibly you were unaware that Hollis has given notice to everyone that his team will be the winners."

Tim glanced at Pamela. "There's your nice Hollis for you," he said.

"Tim, don't be unkind," Pam countered. "You're waging your battle in your way. Hollis has his."

"Since when was bragging part of a battle plan?"

"Why the young shepherd David did just that before he faced Goliath," Pam countered.

"I believe David's remarks were confident answers to the one who was the big braggart, Goliath himself."

"Pardon me," Sybil broke in, "I didn't mean to start a fuss right here in your bedchamber. Perhaps we'd better go, Pamela."

"Tim," Pam went on, "you should also know that the O'Bannons have close relatives in Natchez who own a large cotton plantation."

Suddenly, Tim felt warm in spite of the chill in his room. "Is that a fact?"

Sybil gave a charming smile and nodded. "That is a fact. There are a great number of slaves at Beckworth Manor, and there have been for many years. My cousins were brought up at the knee of their loving black mammy. All the Beckworth slaves love their owners as the owners love their slaves. Each slave is lovingly cared for."

Tim had no idea how to answer. Her words were like a spoonful of molasses, thick and much too sweet. Sweet enough to make a person gag. In his mind he saw big Cloman walking in chains across the wilds of Africa. Then he imagined him dressed in a black suit, opening a carriage door for his master. It was an unsettling thought.

"Excuse me, ladies, but I really must get back to my work," Tim said, closing the conversation. He didn't want to hear another word. He could see that in Sybil's opinion, his stand against slavery was a judgment against her Mississippi kinfolk.

The next morning, Tim got to school early and distributed the carefully copied notes to his teammates. As class began, Mr. Rohmer announced that Mr. Cole's class would also be attending the debate.

Tim felt his throat go dry as paper. He'd finally found his place within his class. He'd gained his classmates' respect as he continued to succeed in spite of everything Hollis did to torment him. Ward's lessons were taking root. But the younger class? That was a different story. Hollis could have them in the palm of his hand within moments.

By two-thirty all the seventh-graders were packed into the classroom. Some sat in seats with eighth-graders. Others stood in the aisles and at the back of the room. The air felt stifling.

Tim began the deep breathing that Ward had taught him and turned his mind to other things. Since there was nothing he could do about the added students in the room, he would have to rise above it.

Isaac was appointed to give their team's opening remarks. True to his nature, Hollis did what he could to unnerve Isaac. Isaac, however, was oblivious. At one point when Hollis was whispering, Isaac looked up from his notes, paused, glared at Hollis, and waited until the boy was quiet. Oh, how Tim wished he had that kind of nerve.

Ward had been right about the opposing team having to rely on financial facts. Everything hinged on business, commerce, and how the abolition of slavery would cause America's economy to collapse. Special emphasis was placed on how the collapse of the Southern economy would affect the steamboat industry. Evidently that was inserted for Tim's benefit, since his family relied heavily on the success of steamboats and steamboat trade.

Tim's team, on the other hand, presented gut-wrenching stories that he had gleaned from Ward's friends and neighbors. Tim noticed tears in the eyes of some of the girls.

Due in part to Ward's training, Tim was able to speak clearly and to look into the eyes of his listeners. He avoided looking at Hollis. Instead, he concentrated on those seventh-graders who sat around him, the ones stifling snickers as Hollis tried various ways to keep them laughing.

At last they were down to the closing remarks. After Hollis had presented his closing statement, the air in the room fairly tingled with tension. Just as Tim was ready to be called to give his closing statement, Isaac raised his hand and asked to be excused.

Tim groaned inwardly. What a time for his friend to take a trip to the necessary! Panic rose in his throat. He needed Isaac there. His friend's presence through the course of the afternoon had meant more than Tim was willing to admit. Back to the deep breathing.

Silence hung thick in the room. There was no snickering now. Even Hollis had become more serious.

Tim was called up. He fixed his mind on the escaped slave he'd met who'd showed the whip scars on his back and arms. And the crippled black girl whose leg had been broken by her master to punish her for running away. She'd managed to escape anyway. With these images in his mind, Tim threw himself into the closing remarks.

Just as he spoke his last line, there was a terrible clanking noise at the door. In walked Isaac with a shackle on his left leg, to which was attached a heavy chain. In his hand rested a weighted lead ball that was attached to the end of the chain.

All eyes turned to stare at the sight. The girls screamed, and one fainted.

CHAPTER 8

Shackles!

Tim could not believe his eyes. Where on earth had Isaac found such a thing? As Tim's friend made his way to the front of the room, the weight of the lead became more apparent by his halting movements. For several agonizing moments he just stood there. The girl who had fainted was being given smelling salts by another girl.

"Seventh-graders," Mr. Rohmer was saying, "you may return to your classroom." There was a deep scowl on his face.

Slowly they filed out, but no one could stop staring at the terrible contraption fastened to Isaac's leg. How he had made it through the hallways to the classroom was more than Tim could figure out.

Once the younger students were gone, Mr. Rohmer turned to Isaac. "Sensationalism and demonstration have no place in a debate, Mr. Proctor. Are you aware you have just disqualified your team?"

Isaac leaned down and let the ball fall a short way to the floor. It hit with a terrible thud. "I surmised as much," he said, giving his lopsided grin.

"Timothy, were you at the bottom of this silly stunt?"

Hollis was now snickering.

Isaac spoke up. "Sir, no one knew my plan. I take full responsibility."

Mr. Rohmer was quiet a moment as though sizing up the event. "You two will remain after class. The rest of you are dismissed."

Tim could hardly bear to look at Isaac. After all the hours and hours of hard work. If they were disqualified, did that mean his grade was lost as well? At that moment, his anger toward Isaac nearly matched his anger toward Hollis. He couldn't bring himself to look over at his friend as they stood together before Mr. Rohmer's desk.

"Timothy, did you know about this stunt?"

Again, Isaac answered, "No one knew, sir. I did this on my own."

Mr. Rohmer looked at Tim. "Timothy?"

Tim shook his head. "I had no idea, sir."

"I want to believe that, son. You had a lot at stake here." Mr. Rohmer turned to Isaac. "Whatever possessed you to take matters into your own hands? Are you not aware that a debate is a team effort?"

"Teams are like committees," Isaac quipped. "Bogged down in rhetoric. I feel it's best to go straight to the heart of a matter."

"I see." Mr. Rohmer made a tent of his fingers and tapped them together thoughtfully. "By all rights I should call your parents in for a talk."

Tim felt his heart lurch, but Isaac never batted an eyelash.

"However," Mr. Rohmer went on, "perhaps the loss of the debate will be punishment enough this time. Isaac, you will lose the grade you would have received for the debate. That grade will have to be made up in extra work. I'll decide on that assignment later.

"Timothy, I will take a percentage off your marks because as the captain you are responsible for your members."

"Yes, sir," Tim answered. He knew Mr. Rohmer's words were true, and that only made him more upset at Isaac's silly actions.

"The two of you are dismissed. Now, Isaac, get that unsightly thing out of here."

Isaac turned to Tim. "Will you help me with this?" He knelt down to unfasten the wire that held the shackle tight. Tim could see then how he'd created a makeshift fastener to secure the band on his ankle.

"You came in with it, you can get out with it," Tim said, not bothering to hide the disgust in his voice. "I'll get your cloak." He turned to go to the cloakroom, where he retrieved both their cloaks.

Once they were out in the hall, Isaac staggering along with the weight in his hands, Tim asked, "Isaac, how could you? I trusted you. I thought you were my friend."

"I am your true friend," Isaac answered.

"How can you say that? We lost the debate."

Isaac stopped in front of the stairway. "Timothy, my good man, on paper Hollis may have won the debate by disqualification. But believe me, the sight of this ball and chain won the debate hands down. After all, isn't that what you wanted? Or was winning the debate more important than convincing your listeners?"

Tim wasn't sure what he thought. "Come on," he said, turning down the stairs. "It's late."

Because of the snow, Pamela was waiting just inside the front door for Tim. And as he had expected, Hollis was standing close to her. No doubt he'd told her the whole story in his words and in his way. Suddenly Tim felt weary and beaten.

"For shame, Isaac," Pamela said, staring at the contraption he carried. "How could you do such a thing?"

"I didn't do this, Pamela," he quipped, cocking an eyebrow. "Someone else designed and created this instrument of torture."

"That's not what I meant, and you know it."

"Here," he said stepping toward her, "want to feel how heavy it is?"

Pamela gave a little shriek and stepped backward, nearly knocking Hollis over.

"No? Then how about you, Hollis. Here, you lift it. How would you like to run through the woods shackled with this and have bloodhounds on your heels?"

Hollis's face grew white, and Tim was afraid the boy might faint like the girl in their class had done earlier. "Isaac," Tim said, "aren't you about finished with your theatrics for today?"

Hollis made his feeble good-byes to Pamela and hurried on his way. After he was gone, Tim helped Isaac into his cloak before they stepped out into the snowy afternoon. "Where are you going with that thing?" Tim wanted to know.

"Back to the jail where it came from."

Tim was incredulous. "You mean it didn't come from an escaped slave?"

"Now did you hear me say such a thing?"

Tim had to laugh in spite of himself. "No, I didn't."

"Can I help what everyone thought?"

"How did you get it from the jailer?"

"I told them it was for a drama at school, and he let me have it. I brought it over last evening after dark and hid it in the bushes just outside the front door."

"Isaac Proctor," Tim said, "you are impossible."

"Yes, well, now I'll work up such a sweat getting this thing back, I'll not even feel this cold air." He grinned. "Who knows? It could have been removed from the leg of an escaped slave. Anything's possible. See you tomorrow, Tim, my friend."

Tim could only shake his head at the sight of Isaac walking through the snow, struggling beneath the weight of the ball and chain. As he walked home with Pamela, Tim realized Isaac had gone to all that trouble and risk for him. And all this time Tim had thought Isaac didn't care about important issues. He'd been wrong.

After a time of silence, Pamela said, "So Isaac Proctor ruined the debate for you. And after all your hard work."

"Did Hollis tell you that?"

"I heard that the seventh-grade girls were aghast at his brashness."

"Perhaps all of Cincinnati could do with a generous dose of Isaac's brashness," Tim said thoughtfully.

Later, when Tim recounted the events of the debate to Ward, he was surprised to see Ward smile. "I'll have to meet this young friend of yours, Tim. He would make an incredible abolitionist. Something like Benjamin Lundy perhaps."

Tim thought about that a moment. He'd heard about the tireless efforts of Lundy, who published the small newspaper with a big name: *The Genius of Universal Emancipation.* This white man had walked all over the nation to spread the news of freedom for black slaves.

"Remember what I said to you about lighting the fire in your classmates?" Ward asked.

"I remember."

"I believe you have done this with Isaac."

Timothy thought about Ward's comment. At first he'd seen Isaac's actions as a mere prank. A joke. Perhaps he'd been too hasty in his judgment.

"At what expense did Isaac present this piece of 'evidence'?"

"His entire grade in elocution. But," he added quickly, "Isaac cares little about his grades."

Ward nodded. "Easy to say. Don't forget he also risked his friendship with you. Had you been greatly angered, you might not have forgiven him. That's a high price."

"I was angry. Very angry."

"And now?"

"Not so angry anymore. I believe I've learned a few lessons from this whole debate."

"It's good to learn from those about us, Tim. Watch people closely, and listen. Listen to what they say, but more importantly, listen to what they don't say."

The admonition sounded confusing. "I'll try," Tim promised.

In spite of Pamela's constant cajoling, Tim turned down invitations to accompany the family to the many holiday festivities about town. The formal gatherings were such a bore, with all the small talk and dancing, and Tim hadn't taken time to learn the newest steps.

"If you continue to stay home all the time, you'll disgrace us," Pamela told Tim. "You said that after the debate you'd not be so burdened with work. That you could have fun again."

Tim knew that part of the problem was that Pam's ideas and his ideas of fun were totally different. One bright, cold Saturday afternoon a few days earlier, Isaac and Tim had hitched a pair of the Proctors' horses to their sleigh, gone up the incline to Mount Ida, and had a great time. Now that was fun!

Though nothing was ever said, Tim sensed that his father didn't care for all the dances and parties either. But Papa went along anyway. Tim wondered if Papa felt he owed it to Mama after all the lean years of their early married life.

Uncle Ben didn't attend the large gatherings either. He told Tim that Emma felt uncomfortable amid such opulence, and some people said cruel things because she was a German girl. Instead, Ben went with Emma to social functions held in the German community.

The night of the O'Bannons' Christmas party, Tim was in the kitchen eating a snack of bread and cheese when the family returned home. Pamela breezed in the door with eyes sparkling and cheeks prettily flushed. Their cloaks were flecked with new-fallen snow. While Papa put the horses away, Willa fussed over Pam and Mama, taking their wraps and offering cups of hot cider.

"My, my, Tim. You should have seen your sister this evening," Mama said. "When I slipped upstairs to the third-floor ballroom, there she was in the midst of the dancing."

Tim had heard Mama and Pam discussing the fact that since Sybil, Pam, and their friends had not yet "come out," another orchestra was hired for them in a ballroom separate from the adults.

"I always did know she would soon turn heads," Tim commented as he closed the book he'd been reading.

"Especially that son of the man who owns the jewelry store. What's his name? What a fine dancer he is."

Tim gave Pam a withering look. "You're speaking of Hollis Bodley?" he asked.

"Oh, yes," Mama said. "That's the one. Hollis." Then Mama glanced at Tim and her expression changed. "Oh, he's the one. . ."

"Yes, Mama," Tim said. "He's the one with whom I debated." He stood and picked up his book to return to his room.

Mama shook her head. "Well, he certainly seemed like a nice young man."

Papa entered just as Mama finished her sentence and asked, "What young man is being discussed?"

"The Bodley boy," Mama said. "The one who paid so much attention to our daughter this evening."

Papa nodded in agreement. "Ah, yes. He seems to be a fine young gentleman. Being groomed to take over his father's business, as I understand it."

Tim couldn't stand to hear another word. He left them to their reminiscing and went to his room. He didn't want to think of Pamela dancing with Hollis Bodley.

Thankfully Christmas was different from all the social whirl. No stuffy protocol to remember, no one to impress, just family and a table heavy with good food. Tim was pleased that

Christmas dinner that year was to be at their house. Their "country cousins," Andrew and Betsy Farley, were expected to come by sleigh from their farm just north of the city. Their children, Rachel, Calvin, and baby Alice, would be with them.

Of course Uncle Ben and Emma would be there as well. All the Lankfords—Uncle Paul and Aunt Ellie and their daughter, Lucy, along with Lucy's betrothed, John Hendricks. Lucy's older brother, George, his wife, Patricia, and their two children—would be coming as well. As Mama called it, a happy houseful!

Betsy Farley was one of Tim's favorite relatives. While she might not be decked out in ruffles, silks, and satins, she appeared not to care. Tim liked her smiling eyes and her easy laughter. Perhaps it was her freedom from the stringent social demands of city life that made her so easygoing.

On Christmas Eve, Tim and his family bundled up and loaded into Papa's elegant new carriage to attend church services with all their guests. During the solemn, reverent service, Tim's thoughts turned to Ward, Clara, and Joseph, and he prayed for their continued safety. From there his mind turned to the untold hundreds and thousands of slaves throughout the land who were in bondage while Tim sat comfortable, warm, and safe in his own home church.

Tim knew Pam was concerned about his serious nature. "You're always scowling," she'd commented to him one day. But he couldn't help it. Something must be done about the problems of slavery, and he wanted to be part of the solution. Getting a law degree from Harvard would give him a way to do that, if only Papa would agree.

Following the Christmas Eve service, everyone gathered at the Allertons' for eggnog and hot cider. The littlest children were bedded down in the back bedroom. In the drawing room, everyone else gathered around the piano and, as Lucy played, they sang carols until they could sing no more. Later, they sat around the open fireplace talking.

Somehow the subject of slavery came up, and Uncle Ben began to tell the group about Tim's debate at school. "I suppose if it were possible, our young Tim would ride through the South, setting free every slave he could find."

This comment drew laughter from the others, almost as though they were laughing about the antics of a small child. A knot formed in the pit of Tim's stomach.

Betsy and Andrew were sitting together on a settee across from where Tim was lounging on the floor near the hearth. For some reason, he happened to glance up at them. They were not laughing.

CHAPTER 9

Slave Catchers

Ward had instructed Tim to listen to what people were not saying. Was this what he meant? Probably no one else in that crowded room had seen what Tim saw in Betsy's eyes at that moment.

Later, as Papa read the Christmas story and as the entire family prayed together, Tim wondered if he'd been mistaken about what he'd seen. Or perhaps he'd misunderstood. Abolition was such a controversial subject, not only in communities, but in homes like theirs. People just couldn't agree.

Later, as he lay awake in his feather bed, listening to the cold north wind whip around their big house, he thought back to the family's conversation that evening. Repeatedly, he'd heard the words "Cincinnati faces South!" As if that explained why an entire race of people should be enslaved. How could money be more important than human lives? It just didn't make sense.

He wondered how his Uncle Ben could have teased him as he had. Had his uncle forgotten what it was like to be teased and humiliated in front of others? When Uncle Ben first came to Cincinnati as an orphan from Boston, the other children had tormented him about his accent and his dapper clothes. But it seemed he'd forgotten all that.

And then there was Tim's own father. Papa had been captured by the British and forced to serve the enemy. How could he have forgotten what it was like to be enslaved?

Lying there, snuggled beneath heavy quilts, Tim resolved that when he became an adult, he would not forget and he wouldn't change his mind from the resolves he now made in his heart.

Christmas morning was joy filled, due in part to the presence of the three Farley children. The giggling and clamor of children as they emptied their stockings and opened gifts made the entire house cheerier. By midmorning, the Lankfords had arrived as well, and once again the house was filled with people.

Thankfully, even though the conversation at dinner turned to abolitionists and pro-slavery groups, at least Tim didn't find himself the brunt of any more jokes. But it disturbed him deeply that the family members agreed that no one had the right to interfere with the business of the Southern slaveholders. "Moreover," Papa said, "no man has a right to separate a slave owner from his property."

Several times, Tim glanced at Betsy and Andrew to gauge their feelings. But their faces showed nothing one way

71

or the other, and they said very little.

Tim had hoped for an opportunity to talk to Betsy and feel her out, but it never came. Since their farm livestock had been left in the care of neighbors, Andrew said they must leave early the next morning. So their short stay was over almost before it had begun. And Tim was left wondering.

The ice on the Ohio River remained thick and hard all through December and January. Ward called it a gift from God, since it served as a highway for scores of slaves escaping from Kentucky in the dark of night.

However, the increase in the number of fugitives meant an increase in the number of slave catchers. On many occasions, Tim would see a motley group of rough-looking men riding into town. Inevitably, they would head for a hotel or tavern. While their clothing looked mangy and their blanket coats somewhat frayed, the powerful Hawken rifles slung into the saddles appeared to be brand new, which meant, of course, that the slave holders who had hired these men were also supplying them with the firearms to do their job. The very thought made Tim cringe.

Slave catchers had one purpose in mind—to return an escaped slave to the owner and collect a fat wad of bounty money. The one thing slave catchers hated was to go home empty handed. When the slave they were chasing suddenly disappeared while the trail was still hot, the angry, frustrated men would grab any black person to take back with them.

The horror stories of slave catchers kidnapping free blacks were growing daily, not just in Cincinnati, but in many places in the North. Tim read about the cases in the pamphlets and abolitionist newspapers that he read almost daily. The thought of a free black person being taken into slavery was almost worse, in Tim's mind, than the slavery itself. Yet these blacks had no protection in a court of law because they weren't allowed to testify.

Tim was riding to Ward's home one gray January afternoon when he saw a telltale group of five horses in front of the Columbian Inn. New rifles were slung into the saddles. He hoped they would quickly take care of business and leave the city.

As he and Ward worked together that day, Tim noticed that Ward seemed unusually distracted. Finally, Tim asked if something was wrong.

Ward gave a wry smile. "Ah, Tim. You're learning to do as I said, aren't you? Listening to what a person doesn't say."

Tim nodded. "I don't usually see you look so worried."

"Slave catchers," he said, his face grim. "They rode into the area last night. I stood my ground and chased them off. But I fear they'll be back again. Everyone's jumpy."

"Can't somebody do something?" Tim didn't see how strangers could come into a community and simply snatch its citizens away without anyone lifting a finger to help.

Ward looked at Tim quietly. He didn't need to say anything. Tim knew.

Upon leaving Ward's house, Tim rode back through town and noticed the horses were no longer at the hotel. He turned Fearnaught to go downhill toward the landing and rode up and down several snow-covered streets until finally he saw them. It was just as he'd surmised—the five horses were now hitched in front of a tavern. After dark, when they were quite drunk, they'd probably head back into Little Africa.

Deep in thought, Tim rode back through town to Isaac's house. He found his friend out at the Proctor stables, which were nearly twice as large as the Allerton stables.

"Hello, Tim," Isaac greeted him. "What brings you here on a cold afternoon? Shouldn't you be home eating your supper?" As Tim came to where Isaac was grooming one of the thoroughbreds, Isaac said, "It doesn't appear to be a social call. What a serious look on that face of yours."

"Isaac, what do you think about free blacks?"

Isaac placed the brush back in the tack box in the corner of the stall. "I used to not think much about anything until I chummed around with you. Now I think too much about everything."

"Are they free or aren't they?"

"I guess I'd say they should be free, but I know public opinion doesn't truly support that. What're you wooling about in that mind of yours?"

"I have reason to believe a bunch of slave catchers may go into Little Africa tonight looking for someone to take back across the river with them."

Isaac's mischievous blue eyes lit up. "You think we could do something about it?"

"Do you?"

"It'll be dark early. Come back here after supper. We can saddle up Quincey and decide what to do from there."

After supper, Tim rode out with Fearnaught to the Proctors' home. The first thing he and Isaac had to do was locate the slave catchers. Tim led the way back into town to the tavern where he'd seen the horses. The horses were no longer there, but it didn't take long to find them. The men had simply moved to a different tavern.

Leaving their horses a couple streets away, the two boys quietly crept up to the tavern and quickly removed the percussion caps from each of the five rifles. While the horses nickered some, the music and laughter coming from inside gave them excellent cover.

Once they returned to their own horses, Isaac said, "What now?"

"We go to Little Africa and wait."

"What makes you sure those catchers will go there?"

"It's not too hard to figure out."

"And what if they take someone? What then?"

Tim thought a moment as they guided their horses across town to Western Row and then south to the black neighborhood. "You know that place downriver a ways where the rocks break the current?"

"You mean where the ice is weakest?"

"That's the place." Tim could barely see his friend's face in the glow of the gas lamp by the side of the street, but he could tell Isaac was grinning. Both boys knew what they were about to do.

"I don't want Ward to know we're here," Tim said as they drew close to his friend's house. "He'd make us go home."

Isaac nodded.

They found an empty shack down the street from Ward's house. Taking the horses around to the back, Tim told Isaac to go inside and watch through the front window.

"What're you gonna do?"

"Find some rocks."

In a few minutes, Tim joined Isaac at the window and handed him several large rocks. "Put these in your pockets. This is all the ammunition you'll have."

Isaac smiled. "Great."

They didn't have long to wait. Almost within the hour, the shouts of drunk men could be heard. This time the men didn't ride toward Ward's house, but rather headed down

75

Western Row, closer to the river.

"Come on," Tim said, "we've got to keep them in sight."

Just as they ran outside, a young black man stepped from his house. He was in the wrong place at the wrong time. Instantly, he was caught up by the slave catchers, gagged, put into handcuffs, and slung onto a saddle.

Tim jumped astride Fearnaught. Isaac was on Quincey, right behind him. "Shout and throw the rocks," Tim instructed. "Then we'll turn and ride downriver."

"Lead the way!"

Tim felt the blood pounding in his head as he rode closer to the group. He let loose with a rock that hit one of the slave catchers right between the shoulder blades.

The drunk man yelled like he'd been shot. Isaac hit one on the shoulder. The two boys shouted and yelled at the slave catchers.

Just as all five men had turned about to see what the yelling was about, Tim yanked on the reins to turn Fearnaught downriver.

"Let's get 'em," one man yelled.

"Naw," called out another. "It's just kids. Let 'em go. Get on across the river."

Isaac turned about in the saddle and let another rock fly. Another dead aim. Now the men were angry and in pursuit. Tim could hear terrible curse words as the men tried to fire their useless rifles.

The farther downriver they rode, the thicker grew the trees and brush. For a few moments, clouds parted and moonlight shone on the icy river. It had been a while since Tim had ridden this way. He hoped he could remember just where the rock formation was located. But Isaac knew exactly where it was.

"They're on our heels," Isaac said. "Turn into the brush just as you get to the edge."

Tim knew they had to be ready either to grab the black man or to fish him out of the river. Jerking Fearnaught to a stop at the river's edge, he jumped down and pulled the horse into the trees just as the first slave catcher rushed by. Tim heard a horrifying cracking noise as the weak ice gave way beneath the weight of the horse. In their drunken state, none of the men who followed him could grasp what had happened. They all headed straight for the broken ice.

"Now!" Isaac cried. Together, Tim and Isaac reached out, grabbed the leg of the cuffed black man, and pulled. He hit the ground with a rough thud as the last horse fell into the frigid water.

CHAPTER 10

To Natchez

Tim and Isaac worked quickly to pull the gag from the man's mouth and then helped him up on Fearnaught's back. Behind them they could hear the screams of the men in the water. Tim shivered at the frightening sounds.

"We're taking you to Ward Baker's," Tim whispered.

The man nodded. Tim saw relief and gratefulness written in his dark eyes.

They tied their horses in back of Ward's house and tapped on the kitchen door. A shocked Clara opened the door.

"Timothy! What's happened?" Then she saw the cuffs on the man's wrists. "Oh, my goodness! William," she said to the rescued man, "get yourself in here."

Ward was there within seconds, and looking at the trio, he sized up the situation quickly. He smiled at Tim. "I presume this is your friend Isaac Proctor?"

"These here boys saved my life, Mr. Baker," said William. "They led them turr'ble men right into dat river. We done heard 'em hollering and thrashing about in the water."

"Led them to the rocks, did you?" Ward asked.

"Yes, sir," Tim answered. Then he formally introduced Ward to Isaac, and the two shook hands.

"Did they see you?" Clara asked with an edge to her voice.

"Ma'am," Isaac said, "they were so sopping drunk, they didn't see much of anything. It was black as ink out there."

To William, Isaac said, "I hope we didn't hurt you when we pulled you off the horse."

William, who wasn't much older than his rescuers, gave a wide grin and rubbed his backside. "It smarted some, but it was plenty worth it."

Tim saw the satisfied look on Isaac's face and knew Ward had been right about lighting a fire inside him.

"We'll take care of William now," Ward told them. "You two get out of here and get on home. And don't take Western Row. Go out the back streets and take the long way around."

They did just as Ward suggested, choosing the streets where there were the fewest lights. Before the boys parted, Tim thanked Isaac for helping. Then Tim asked, "Do you think any of the slave catchers drowned?"

Isaac shook his head. "First of all their screams could be heard all the way to the landing. Someone was sure to hear and come running. And second, that ice is so heavy I feel sure they could crawl up on it."

"Even drunk?"

Isaac laughed. "Nothing like a little ice water to sober up a drunk."

The next day word was all over town about the slave catchers who were so drunk they'd crossed the Ohio at the wrong point and nearly drowned. Isaac had been right, men from the landing had helped pull them out. Last seen, they were crossing where the ice was firm, back to Kentucky empty-handed.

Most people in Cincinnati were overjoyed to have a "Westerner" elected as their new president. Andrew Jackson was not only a common man from the frontier, but also a slaveholder. Tim had seen booklets describing Jackson's large plantation, Hermitage.

After the ice floes broke up in late February, the entire city turned out on the landing to see the steamboats carrying the newly elected president and his companions.

Tim and Isaac climbed to the roof of the boatworks, which offered the best view. Andrew Jackson came out on the deck of one of the steamboats to wave to the people. Tim could see the wide bands of black crepe on Jackson's top hat and on his sleeve, representing his grief for his beloved wife, Rachel, who had died a short time before. In a few weeks, Mr. Jackson would be sworn in as president. Ward had told Tim that Jackson was much too rambunctious to be a good president.

One afternoon after the president's entourage had passed through, Tim was walking home from school with Pam. She seemed more bubbly than usual.

"I have exciting news," she told him. "I've been invited to travel to Natchez with Sybil and her family. They're going for a visit to the Beckworth plantation."

"After school's out?" he asked.

"No. In mid-March."

"That's only a few weeks away." Tim shook his head. "I don't think Mama and Papa will let you go." He knew how protective Papa was of Pamela. He hardly wanted her out of his sight. Tim looked at his younger sister, dressed in her delicate apricot-colored dress and matching bonnet. Somehow Pam knew the right colors to wear to make her copper curls glow.

"I believe you're right, Tim. And that's why I want you to agree to go."

"Me?" Tim recoiled. "To Natchez? To a plantation?"

She nodded and smiled. "If you go as my escort, Papa will have no qualms about my going. I'm just sure of it." She turned to him then with soulful eyes and added, "You wouldn't want to cause me not to be able to go, would you? Oh please, Tim. I've never been able to travel anywhere, and Sybil has been almost everywhere. This could be my only chance."

"What about school?" Tim couldn't bear the thought of leaving his schoolwork behind.

"Our teachers could give us the assignments to take with us." Pam sounded so sure of herself. "If you go," she added, "then you could see for yourself what caring, sweet people Southerners truly are. They really aren't the monsters you might think they are."

"Give me a day or so to think about it."

Pam smiled. "That I can do. I'm pleased you at least agree to think about it."

When Tim told Ward about the possibility of his taking the trip, Ward said, "By all means go. If you see for yourself, you'll never forget it. You need to see the empire that has been built on the bloodied backs of the black man."

Isaac's reaction was disappointment that he couldn't come along. "My father took me to New Orleans once when I was young," he said, "but I barely remember the trip." Grinning, he added, "We make such a rip snortin' pair together, it's a pity I can't be with you."

"I don't suppose I'd be too good an escort for Pamela if you were there with me," Tim said.

"And I suppose you're right," Isaac retorted.

After hearing these responses, Tim began to think differently about the trip. Two days later, as they were walking home, he told Pam that he would agree to serve as her escort. She was so ecstatic Tim thought she was going to hug him right there on the street in front of everyone.

"Now it's your job to help convince Mama and Papa," she told him.

But Tim knew it wasn't his job. Pamela had her own way of getting what she wanted from Mama and Papa.

As Tim suspected, Pam presented the request during dinner. "Wouldn't it be wonderful for Tim to be able to see what kind, gentle people Southerners truly are?" she argued.

Papa bit the hook. Tim and Pam were going to Natchez, Mississippi.

While other steamboats were built to carry freight and produce, the magnificent steamboat *General Pike* was designed especially for passengers, with elegant staterooms and a large formal dining room. Since nothing but the best would do for the O'Bannon family, *General Pike* was the boat they were taking to Natchez.

The name was scrolled in large blue letters on the white sides of the boat. Delicate, ornately carved woodwork gave the boat a lacy wedding cake appearance. Twin black fluted smokestacks pointing skyward contrasted against the stark white of the boat.

Tim was dressed in his new top hat of soft gray, which matched his gray swallowtail coat. Mama had seen to it that he was fitted with a suitable wardrobe for the trip. While he didn't think all the fuss was necessary, he didn't have much to say about the matter.

As usual, the landing was a hectic mass of noise and confusion. Wagons and carts full of freight waited to be loaded, as well as carriages that were delivering passengers. Men shouted, and crates, barrels, and boxes were carried up the gangplank. Mama and Papa came to see them off, and Papa gave Tim stern warning to behave like a gentleman and to look after his sister. He promised he would.

Sybil's father, Roger O'Bannon, was a serious man with a plump front and smooth-shaven round face. He wore a monocle, which he removed from his eye and tapped nervously on his hand as he talked. Mrs. O'Bannon fluttered about and twittered a great deal.

Although Tim would never be as giddy as the girls, still he felt a chill of excitement as the steam engines began their chugging noise and the deep-throated whistle sounded. Presently, well-wishers were asked to leave the boat, and the gangplank was pulled up. Pam waved and called out goodbye to Mama and Papa as the sidewheel began turning.

Ropes were loosened, and slowly the boat moved from the landing to the center of the Ohio to begin the journey southward. Tim watched as the large buildings along the landing became smaller and smaller in the distance, especially the four-story building with the large sign "Lankford & Allerton Boatworks" painted in bold red on the side.

Tim was thankful he was to have his own private stateroom. That meant he could study in peace. He'd been concerned about being out of school, but Mr. Rohmer had assured him he could keep up. "The education you'll receive on such a trip cannot be found in books," the teacher had said.

As Tim was organizing his books and papers in his room, a tap sounded on the adjoining door. "Tim? It's me, Pam. May I come in?"

"It's open."

Pam, having removed her bonnet, cape, and gloves, appeared relaxed and happy. "Aren't the staterooms charming? Every comfort of home," she said.

He nodded as he lifted his satchel and set it on the bed. "Charming," he agreed.

"I just wanted to thank you for agreeing to come," she continued. "I don't believe I'd be here otherwise."

"You're welcome." Tim smiled at her as he pulled schoolbooks from his bag and lined them neatly in the drawer of the small wall desk.

Eyeing the books, she said, "I hope you're not planning to stay cooped up in here studying the whole time."

"Maybe not the whole time," he teased.

"Tim, please remember we're guests of the O'Bannons. Might I ask you to be more civil to my friend Sybil?"

Tim looked up at Pam. "To Sybil?"

"Why, yes. Perhaps you could sit by her side at supper this evening."

"Why?"

Pam moved into the small room and sat down in the upholstered chair by the window. "My dear brother," she said with a little laugh, "haven't you noticed that you are a handsome fellow? If you haven't, be assured others have."

Tim felt his face growing warm. Sybil notice him? What a bizarre notion. Boys with suave good looks like Isaac Proctor's brought attention from the girls.

Pam laughed as she saw Tim's discomfort. "If your head weren't buried in books so much, you might see what's going on about you."

"I see what's going on," he said.

Pam rose to her feet. "Only partially, Timothy. Only partially." She stepped to the door. "Will you do as I asked?"

Tim wondered what he would have to say to a girl whose kinfolk owned slaves. But he did want to do right by his sister. "I suppose I could consider sitting by her side. But only if you are on my other side."

Slipping out the door into her own room, Pam smiled and said, "It's agreed."

CHAPTER 11

Beckworth Manor

Although it was extremely awkward at first, Tim did as he had promised. In the elegant, carpeted dining room, he sat by Sybil and talked with her. Soon he realized there were issues and subjects to discuss other than slavery. When Sybil wasn't giggling, she appeared to have a rather smart head on her shoulders.

The days were calm and peaceful, and the weather held good. Each day was a smidgeon warmer than the one before as they followed the Ohio to where it joined the mighty Mississippi. Tim's favorite pastime, next to studying, was to stand at the rail and watch the green walls of forest float leisurely by. Here and there small hamlets appeared, and sometimes a cabin could be seen through the trees. The farther they traveled on the serene waterways, the more his worries and concerns seemed to melt away.

At one point, the captain learned that Tim was related to the Lankford and Allerton boatbuilders and invited him to visit the pilot house. The pilot's view of the majestic river proved even grander than that from the passenger deck. Tim could sense the life of the river and its ever-changing moods.

"She's a persnickety cat," explained the captain. "Purring and calm one moment, snorting and clawing the next. She demands my full respect." He smiled. "And I'm proud to give it to her."

Late one evening, the *General Pike's* deep steam whistles sounded as they approached the landing docks at Memphis, Tennessee. Most of the passengers turned out on deck whenever a large city was approached. Tim was standing at the rail with Pam on the upper deck as the boat slowed its big engines and smoothly slipped up to the landing. Bright chatter and laughter sounded among the group as they watched passengers leaving and new ones boarding.

Then, down a Memphis street, something caught Tim's attention. In the distance marched a line of five black men in leg chains, each linked to the other. In spite of the warm evening, Tim's skin went cold.

No one else seemed to notice them. The conversations droned on around him, but he saw only the men dressed in tatters, with their heads bowed, shuffling slowly toward the boat. The sound of clinking chains became audible as they approached. Led by two white men, they crossed the gangplank. They were coming onboard. Slaves right on the boat with him. Tim could scarcely believe it.

That night after dark, he took a walk on the lower deck. In his pocket he had one of the pamphlets printed by the abolitionist Quaker, Mr. Lundy. Tim soon located the slaves near the engines. They were forced to sleep on the hard deck with no protection from the cold. Tim strolled slowly back and forth twice, attempting to determine if they were being guarded. He saw no one. There weren't any windows by the noisy engines, either.

Taking a deep breath, Tim walked closer to the men. One slave looked up at him with fear in his eyes. The others, leaning against one another, were asleep. Tim pulled the pamphlet from his pocket.

"Here," he said softly, yet loud enough to be heard over the noise of the engines. "Take this. I'm a friend."

The man shook his head, his eyes wide. "No, no! Trouble with Massa iffin' he catches me! Them slaves what reads is whipped."

"You're not to read?"

The man shook his head again. "No, suh. And 'sides that, I cain't read nohow."

Their voices awakened the others. Tim looked at the other frightened faces. He felt rather foolish. It had never occurred to him that slaves couldn't read. Ward had probably read more books than Timothy had ever seen, and he taught others in Little Africa how to read.

The slave at the far end, however, calmly held out his hand. Tim moved to him and put the pamphlet in his hand.

"Don't do it, Silas," the other man warned. "It be trouble for all of us."

But the man said nothing. He folded the pamphlet as tiny as he could, then rolled it up in the pants leg of his frayed trousers. He smiled again, and Tim went on his way.

Natchez-Under-the-Hill, Tim had been told, was the most

sordid spot along the river. It was home to riffraff such as rough boatmen, indigents, and criminals. But high on the bluffs above the river sat the palatial mansions of the wealthy merchants. The two sets of people seldom, if ever, met.

Two smart open carriages were on hand to whisk the guests away to the Beckworth plantation. Mrs. O'Bannon flitted about, fussing over all the trunks and bags to make sure nothing was left onboard. Mr. O'Bannon stood by and puffed on a long cigar.

Tim studied the impeccably dressed black livery men who drove the carriages and carried the trunks and bags. A wagon, also driven by a uniformed black driver, sat in readiness to transport the larger trunks.

Soon they were loaded and on their way. The ride took them through the town of Natchez and out into the countryside, where they traveled through winding back roads among stately live oaks, dripping with gray Spanish moss. Pamela gasped at every turn, as another new scene came into view.

Tim had steeled himself against being impressed by the plantations, but it was useless. Natchez itself was made up of a number of showy homes, but out in the countryside, the plantation homes were even more opulent and elegant in design. Each one seemed to be larger and more palatial than its neighbor.

Late in the afternoon the day grew quite warm. The ladies' parasols were up, and Tim was wishing he could shed his coat. He was amazed as he thought of frost still covering the ground each morning in Cincinnati. The dense forest gave shade, providing some relief, but not much. Suddenly the carriages broke out of the forested area to a clearing where newly planted cotton fields stretched out endlessly in every direction.

"It's right over this next hill," Sybil said to Pam. "Wait till you see it. And just wait till you meet all my cousins. They're ever so much fun. Over there," she said, pointing.

Pam and Tim craned about to see. There, spread out on a green knoll surrounded by graceful shade trees and scarlet rhododendrons in full bloom, sat Beckworth Manor. Tall white columns rose up the full three stories of the house, supporting ornate balconies on the second and third floors. A sweeping veranda surrounded the entrance. Lower wings spread out gracefully from both sides of the main house.

The carriages, followed by the wagon, turned off the road to follow a tree-lined lane. Quail whirred up, and meadowlarks warbled a sweet welcome. Sweet scents from flowers filled the air. Tim could see vast vegetable gardens, barns, and sheds. The smaller houses set among the fields, he later learned, were where the overseers lived. Tim never dreamed a plantation would be so beautiful.

The carriages pulled right up to the front steps of the big house. A number of other empty carriages stood about in the shade of a grove of walnut trees. Sybil explained that every time they came to visit, the Beckworths invited their neighbors from miles around to join in the festivities.

Glancing at Tim, she added, "They'll no doubt have a cotillion this evening." Then she smiled coyly and looked away.

Tim cringed. At home he could easily have stayed in his room, but how would he escape here?

He carried his satchel of books as he followed the others up the steps into the grand marbled entryway of the house. In the center, twin curved staircases rose up to a wraparound balcony. He could tell from Pam's expression that she was in awe. He was in awe as well.

The house was teeming with guests, and even after introductions, Tim had difficulty determining who were guests and who were the Beckworth family members. They were shown to their rooms by the black housemaids, dressed in starched white dresses and aprons, with white scarves wrapped about their heads.

Later in the afternoon, the young people were to take lemonade in the large gazebo in the garden at the rear of the house. There he and Pamela came to know Sybil's three cousins: Danette, the youngest at eleven; dark-haired Ramona, who was the age of Pam and Sibyl; and then the eldest, Jack, who was fifteen.

Several other guests were there as well, including a lovely girl named Malvina Dorchester. Tim knew immediately that Pam was quite taken with this eighteen-year-old young woman, and he watched as his sister hung on Malvina's every word.

Tim shyly hung back, not wanting to become entangled in the conversations that were flying back and forth. Jack Beckworth asked him a couple polite questions in his soft southern drawl. But after sensing little response from Tim, Jack moved on to other guests. Eventually, Tim was able to slip away and stroll through the flower-filled gardens.

He followed brick walkways down winding shady paths till he came to a stone bench beneath an ancient sprawling live oak. Sitting down, he had time to collect his thoughts. Hummingbirds flitted in and out of the heavy honeysuckle vines. Through the trees and shrubbery, he had a clear view of the big house as it sat majestically in the center of all it possessed. The empire, he thought, remembering Ward's words. The empire built on the bloodied backs of black men. It was much more powerful than he'd ever imagined.

Tim tried his best to avoid the cotillion that evening, but Pam began to scold much as Mama would have done if she'd been there. Pam had already scolded him for slipping away from the garden party.

"Jack and Ramona were going to take you to the dance master and have him show you a few steps, but no one could find you," she'd said in a huff. Hearing this, Tim was even more pleased that he'd left the scene. Just then, the dinner bell rang, and Tim escorted Pam to the elaborate dining room.

After dinner, Pam stood in Tim's room, scolding once again as he tried to duck out of going to the dance. She insisted he had no choice but to attend the cotillion.

"I hope you can see now the importance of knowing how to dance," she continued. "Mama says she's sorry she didn't insist that you learn long ago, before. . ."

"Before I became so melancholic." He finished the sentence for her. "I know, Pam. I've heard Mama say those words."

"Look here," she said giving a little twirl. "The quadrille is frightfully simple, and the contradance even simpler. I'll show you the rudiments, but then you're on your own."

Pam, obviously wanting to save her brother from total disgrace, took about an hour to show him a few basic steps, then left to get ready. As she slipped out the door, she turned to say, "And the sweet black girl named Lizzie will be helping Sybil and me dress. Tim, she's the nicest thing you ever met in all your days."

Tim's insides wrenched at her words. How could she? When offered a room steward upon arrival, Tim had quickly turned down the service. Although brows were raised, Tim figured he could still dress himself.

At precisely half past eight, he was dressed in his green tailcoat and linen trousers. Although he'd struggled some with tying his cravat, it was passable. Straightening his stiff upturned collar, he glanced in the mirror above the washstand, ran the hairbrush one more time through his dark curls, and deemed himself ready.

Out the door and down the hall, he tapped on Pam's door, which was answered by the black girl named Lizzie. She gave Tim a bright smile. "My stars, Missy Pamela's brother is near to bein' purty as his sister."

Tim blushed as he heard Sybil giggling in the background. He hadn't thought about Sybil being in Pam's room. They obviously had wanted to get ready together. The two girls looked like grown women in their full brocade dresses with large puffed sleeves. Pam's copper hair had been plaited in a high chignon with curls hanging about her face. Tim was almost sure she'd added color to her cheeks and lips, but he'd never tell Mama.

As the girls came out into the hall, they were joined by Sybil's cousins and several other young people. Together, they descended the wide staircase. The ballroom was situated at the far end of the west wing, but the music from the stringed orchestra filtered sweetly throughout the house. Southern customs allowed twelve- and thirteen-year-old girls to dance with the adults, which thrilled Pam to no end.

When they arrived, the ballroom was already crowded with dancers and other guests, along with the black house stewards who deftly moved among the crowd, carrying silver trays. Tim tried not to stare at the gleaming chandeliers hanging from the ceiling or at the polished golden dance floor.

93

French countryside scenes filled the ornate wallpaper, making Tim want to step up and touch it to see if it were real.

The rhythm of the lively music set his toe to tapping, and after dutifully joining in a quadrille or two, he found it rather easy to catch on. He had to admit it was good fun.

Pam began to tease him that several of the lovely Southern belles were eyeing him. Both the quadrille and the contradance allowed that partners change often, which prevented his dancing with the same partner for long. Then the orchestra changed the rhythm, and the dance floor was cleared except for several couples who were either betrothed or married.

"This is what I was telling you, Pam," Sybil said in excited whispers. "It's called the waltz. Mama calls it scandalous, but I think it's perfectly wonderful."

Tim watched as the couples faced one another. The man put his gloved hand on the lady's back, and his other hand lightly held his partner's hand. As the gentlemen stepped out, the couples began to twirl about the room in step with a one-two-three rhythm. Tim could readily see why Mrs. O'Bannon deemed the waltz scandalous. He decided to take that moment to slip out the side door to the veranda.

CHAPTER 12

Slave Quarters

For a time, Tim leaned against the veranda railing and breathed deeply of the soft fragrances of the warm night. The fresh air felt better than the stuffy ballroom. In the moonlight, he studied the sloping lawn and masses of shrubs and waxy-leafed magnolia trees. He tried to imagine what the land had looked like when John Beckworth first arrived over forty years ago. Tim had heard Jack boast that his grandfather had carved the plantation from the dense forest and heavy undergrowth.

Moving away from the sounds of the dancing and music, Tim went down the steps and followed a path past the gazebo where they'd been that afternoon. Suddenly he heard another sound. He thought it was music, but it sounded more like the low humming of a hundred bumblebees. What was it?

Past the gate at the far edge of the garden, he found a winding dirt road that led into the trees. Though it was darker, still the brilliant moon lit the way. The sounds were clearer now. It was singing. The road led to a small clearing where a group of shabby log cabins sat in two facing rows. Tim's breath caught in his throat. Of course! He'd found the slave quarters. The song, sung in simple harmony with rich tones, came floating on the warm night air:

> Swing low, sweet chariot
>   Comin' fo' to carry me home.
> Swing low, sweet chariot
>   Comin' fo' to carry me home.

The song was haunting, as though it wrapped the slaves together in their plight.

Quietly, Tim moved from the road into the darkness of the trees from where he could get a better look but not be seen. Small fires burned in front of the cabins, and groups of slaves sat around the fires. Others sat on the broken-down steps. Some of the fires had tripods over them from which kettles hung. Half-naked children laughed and ran among the grown-ups.

The tumbledown shacks made the houses in Little Africa seem like mansions. He couldn't imagine these cabins standing after a strong windstorm.

Just then, a tall muscular man emerged from one of the cabins. Tim recognized him as one of the drivers he'd seen that morning. But instead of wearing an impeccable uniform, he wore the barest of rags. Tim shook his head at the pitiful sight. How he wished he had a handful of his pamphlets.

Suddenly, a strong, heavy hand clapped down on Tim's shoulder. Tim froze.

"What do you think you're doing out here?" came the gruff voice. Tim turned to see one of the plantation overseers with a coiled whip in his hand. A wide-brimmed hat threw a shadow across his face. "What business do you have out here?" he growled.

"None, sir." Tim struggled to get his wits about him. "I was just taking a walk and heard the singing."

"Just heard the singing." The man sneered. "You Yankees are all alike. Sneaky. Can't trust a one of you. Come with me. We'll see what Mr. Beckworth has to say about this."

Tim was taken through the back door of the big house, down a long hallway to a mahogany-paneled office. There he was told to wait until Mr. Beckworth could be brought. Unfortunately, when Mr. Beckworth came into the office, he was accompanied by Mr. O'Bannon.

Though embarrassed, Tim explained to the men that he was merely taking a walk and became turned around. Tim didn't really care whether they believed him or not. He'd seen the slave quarters for himself, and that was all that mattered.

In a cold stern voice, Mr. Beckworth ordered Tim to stay far away from the slave quarters during the remainder of his stay.

Pam was mortified when she learned what had happened. "Why can't you simply enjoy the hospitality of our hosts and behave yourself?" she demanded. Tim had no answer for her.

A few days later, all the young people were playing shuttlecock and battledores on the lawn. It was a game Tim had played often in the schoolyard at Danenhower. He joined in the fun for a time, batting his feathered ball and keeping it in the air for more times even than Jack.

After a while, he decided to take a break and sat on the grass in the shade of a magnolia. It was then that Malvina Dorchester came strolling over to him.

"Afternoon, Timothy," she said in a honey-sweet drawl. "Do you mind if I sit with you a moment?" She waved to a stone bench nearby.

Tim looked up at her, wondering why she'd singled him out, since most of the young people were either in the game or gathered at the gazebo.

"You may sit wherever you choose," he said.

Malvina's dark eyes squinted as she laughed at his remark. "Ah, you Yankees. Manners aren't one of your strong suits," she said as she closed her silk parasol and seated herself primly on the bench. "One of our Southern gentlemen would have stood when I approached, and then he would have dusted the bench before allowing me to be seated."

Tim felt his face growing crimson. "If charade is important to you, why approach a Yankee?"

Twirling the parasol in her fingers, she gave another little laugh. "And defensive as well. My, my. What a combination." She shook her head. "It's enough to set a lady's teeth on edge like a sour persimmon."

Tim looked back to the game. Pamela had joined in and was laughing and flirting shamelessly with Jack Beckworth. Tim didn't much like Malvina. Even more, he didn't like Pam to be so taken with all the folderol here at Beckworth, and that included Malvina Dorchester.

"I understand you were caught down at the slave quarters after dark last night. Looking over things, were you?"

Even Mr. Beckworth hadn't been that pointed. "I took a walk and got turned around," Tim said, still watching the game. Pamela had just hit the shuttlecock hard, causing Jack to miss his serve.

"Unmannerly, defensive, and now I must add deceptive as well," Malvina said in an accusing tone. When Tim didn't answer, she added, "I understand this is your first visit to the South. Tell me, Timothy Allerton, what do you think of what we've carved out of the wilderness?"

Timothy thought of how no slaves had been needed to carve Cincinnati out of the wilderness. Not trusting Malvina, he answered, "I don't think much about it either way."

"Come now, Timothy, don't be modest. Sybil tells me you were in a heated debate at your school recently. It was, I believe, on the subject of slavery. Am I correct?"

Blast Sybil anyhow. Tim looked up at Malvina, trying to remember Ward's instructions about holding eye contact. A little breeze fluttered the flowers tucked into her straw bonnet. "That is correct," he answered, keeping his voice steady.

"So then you do think about it."

"Miss Dorchester, you didn't ask me what I thought of slavery."

"Pardon me," she fairly purred. "Let me be more specific. What do you think of slavery?"

"I feel no person should be owned, whether black or white."

"Ooo, my. Strong opinions. Sybil was right." Malvina unfolded her ivory fan and waved it a few times. "The Dorchester plantation, Mulberry Hill, is twenty miles from here. My father owns twice as many slaves as the Beckworths. And all, I might add, are lovingly cared for."

"I can only take your word for that," Tim replied.

"Timothy, I dare say, most every business in your home-town of Cincinnati in some way or other depends upon trade with Southern slaveholders. Even and most especially the steamboat industry."

So she knew his father's trade.

"The fine clothes y'all wear," she went on, "if you stop to consider, are due to the massive wealth of the South." She stood up and opened the ruffled parasol.

Having been reminded of his manners, Tim stood as well.

"Remember this, Mr. Allerton." Malvina's dark eyes fairly snapped as she spoke. "We love all our slaves. We would never treat them as shabbily as you do the blacks in Cincinnati. Why, your councilmen are about to drive the black population out of town. Who knows? It could be happening this very minute."

She turned to go, but over her shoulder, she added, "We Southerners would never do that to our beloved slaves!"

Malvina's strong words rang in Tim's head for the rest of his stay at Beckworth Manor. She was right. He knew she was right, and he hated that she was right. Business built on slavery was so much a part of American life, he wondered if it could ever be broken loose.

The ride on the *General Pike* carrying them back up the Mississippi took longer than coming down. Tim felt impatient and anxious to get back home. He wanted to talk to Ward. To share with him all the details of the trip. And he wanted to make sure Little Africa was still intact. He marveled that a young woman like Malvina knew so much about events in a city so far away. He'd assumed Southern girls thought only about dances and fancy gowns.

He also felt anxious about his studies. It had been impossible to avoid the many social functions at the Beckworths', so now he threw himself back into his schoolwork.

Pam talked constantly about Sybil's cousins and their knowledge of decorum, manners, and social graces. Tim could tell by her voice that she greatly admired the Beckworths and all their finery and was perhaps a bit envious.

Before the trip had progressed three days, Pam was complaining to Tim about his moodiness. She'd come to his room to see why he hadn't joined them at the docking at Greenville.

"Studying again?" she said, looking at the books and paper strewn everywhere. "I thought you were learning to have fun, Tim," she said, shaking her head. "Now look at you."

"There was no time to study before, but now there is. So I'm taking advantage of it."

"Sybil feels you've rebuffed her," Pam added with a pout.

Tim wondered if she'd learned that pout from her new friends down South. "I cannot help how Sybil feels," he answered.

Pam took a breath to argue the point, then heaved a deep sigh. "Timothy Allerton, you're impossible."

The door closed, and Tim went back to his studies.

Spring had arrived in Ohio by the time they arrived home. Flowers were in bloom, and trees had budded out in shades of pale green. Uncle Ben and Emma Schiller, along with Mama and Papa, were at the landing to greet them, and Pam began chattering like a magpie about all she'd seen and heard.

Papa walked by Timothy's side as they carried bags to the waiting carriage. "Well, Son," he said, "I trust this trip has helped you to see things more clearly. The planters aren't what you thought they were."

101

Tim wasn't sure how to answer. Are any of us who we really appear to be? he wondered.

To Tim's surprise, his father had hired a driver for the family carriage. He again thought of Malvina's remarks about their wealth coming from the South and shook his head.

When Tim returned to school, he found he was only slightly behind in his lessons. Hollis seemed more subdued but continued to be intent on besting Timothy in every class and assignment.

In private, Isaac told Tim that things had heated up considerably at city hall. "People's tempers are flaring," he explained.

They were sitting on a bench in the schoolyard eating their lunch on Tim's first day back. "From what I understand, and from the articles in the *Daily Gazette*, it appears to be causing deep division."

"It was that way before I left."

"It's more so now. The election for ward councilmen is coming up, and each man is running on this issue. I'm convinced everyone running in support of the black laws will win."

Tim shook his head. Thinking of Ward and Clara, he could scarcely eat. What would happen to his friends?

Briefly, he shared with Isaac what he'd seen on his journey—the black men chained together on the boat and the run-down shanties of the slave quarters on the plantation. "It's a way of life for the planters, Isaac. They've owned men and women for so long, it seems that even the blacks are duped into thinking it's acceptable."

That evening Tim walked Pam home, then quickly saddled Fearnaught and rode straight to Ward's house. When

102

Clara came to the door, she glanced about nervously. Tim thought she'd be excited to see him after his long absence, but she said, "Put Fearnaught around back, Tim. I'll let you in the kitchen door."

Once Tim was inside, Ward came striding down the hallway toward him. "Tim, my friend," he said with a warm smile. "You're home. How glad we are to see you."

He shook hands with Tim and patted him on the shoulder. "Clara," he said gently. "We'll take tea in my office."

Clara smiled a bit, seeming to come to herself. "We're pleased you're home, Timothy."

Then little Joseph came toddling down the stairs and spied Tim. Now the welcome was complete. Joseph ran to Tim and grabbed him about the legs. "Timo-ty come home," he said. Tim picked him up and swung him toward the ceiling just to hear him laugh.

Later, in Ward's office, Ward apologized for Clara's actions. "She's frightened," he said. "I suppose you've heard the news."

Tim nodded. "Isaac explained."

"I wish it were not so, but Mr. Bodley seems to be one of the more outspoken men. He headed up a committee to create a petition asking city hall to take measures to prevent the increase of the black population in Cincinnati." Ward looked at Tim with steady eyes. "And we can pretty much surmise what 'measures' are to be taken."

Tim shivered. That meant enforcing the dreaded black laws.

"Clara has asked me again if we can leave for Canada."

"I think I agree with her," Tim said.

Ward shook his head. "Not yet. I must organize our resistance to city hall. I'm in the process of raising up black leaders and training them to speak out for their rights." He paused, and then said, "But we can't solve all that here and now. Please, Tim, I want to hear about your trip."

So for the next few minutes, over tea and cake, Tim told of his experiences, describing in detail the wealth and opulence. He told of the incident with the slaves on the boat and his peek at the slave quarters at the plantation. Then he related the conversation he'd had with Malvina.

"Her words were confusing to me, Ward. It made me want to burn my new swallowtail coat. What do you make of her reasoning?"

Ward leaned back in his chair and smiled. "It's called rationalizing, Tim. If she can make you feel you're a part of what they are doing, it eases her conscience. At this point, there's hardly an item one can purchase that is not in some way affected by slavery. But that is not our fault, and it's not because we're not trying to do something about it."

Tim nodded, feeling better. He knew Ward would be able to clear up the confusion.

"Now," Ward asked, "what are you going to do with your new knowledge?"

"I've been thinking about that. I plan to use it as the basis of my speeches in elocution. I have two to make before school lets out in May."

Ward nodded. "Need any help?"

Tim smiled. He felt so happy to be back in Ward's company. "I'll accept all the help I can get."

Before Tim left, Ward asked him to come into Little Africa the back way, to avoid Western Row, and to keep Fearnaught in back of the house. "For Clara's peace of mind," he said. And Tim understood. He understood all too well.

CHAPTER 13

Pam's Birthday

Tim had only thought Pamela was in a social whirl at Christmas time. It paled in comparison to what took place once she returned from Natchez. There were sewing circles, singing school, piano recitals, dancing lessons, and of course parties and balls of one sort or another. Pamela's thirteenth birthday came in May, and there was to be a grand party. She talked of little else.

Tim, meanwhile, concentrated on his final tests at school, especially the speeches. Hollis was heard to say that all abolitionists were lunatics who wanted to destroy the economy of the nation.

"Freeing the slaves would bring the South to her knees,"

105

spouted Hollis. Perhaps if Tim could help the students envision men shackled together in leg chains and little black children with not enough food or clothes, he might change the minds of some of his classmates.

One evening during supper, Papa once again brought up the subject of Tim working at the boatworks during the summer months. "When your studies are not demanding all your time," Papa said.

To everyone's surprise, Tim agreed. The issue didn't matter to him anymore. Previously, he'd feared that working for Papa meant he'd be trapped at the boatworks for the rest of his life. But now he knew that sooner or later, he would study law. Sooner or later he would be prepared to represent those who could not represent themselves. Nothing, but nothing, could stop him.

Ward helped Tim with his last two speeches. One he called "Shackled." The final one he titled "At the Cabin Door." Together, he and Ward combed through abolitionist newspapers and pamphlets for the perfect quotes to support his points.

Tim decided to do what the abolitionist newspapers did. He quoted advertisements from Southern newspapers offering rewards for runaway slaves. Many slaves were described by the scars and wounds that had been given to them by cruel masters. Once all his information was assembled, Tim practiced the speeches, with Ward as his audience of one.

"After you've given the speeches," Ward asked one evening, "then what happens to them?"

Tim studied his friend's face. "I don't understand what you're asking."

"Will they be placed in a drawer and the drawer closed?"

"What else could I do with them?"

Ward held up his book of speeches by James Madison. "What else can one do with a speech?" His words were heavy with meaning.

Tim swallowed. "Publish?"

"Publish."

"Where?"

"Tim, you have a keen mind, and these are excellent speeches. After you've presented them to your class, send a copy of each to the *Liberator*. I feel sure they'll be published."

"You think so?" The idea was both frightening and exhilarating.

"You won't know unless you try."

The speeches were scheduled on different days of the same week. Everyone else in Mr. Rohmer's class had finished their speeches, but Tim was behind due to the trip to Natchez. He could sense a profound difference in his presentations from the beginning of the school year. There probably wasn't a thing Hollis Bodley could do now to distract him. And strangely, Hollis had finally stopped trying.

During each of Tim's presentations, the class was so quiet, one could almost hear the ticking of the large wall clock. One thing Ward had taught him was to use meaningful pauses and not hurry.

"Don't cheat your important points by running over them," Ward would say. "Allow them a few moments to penetrate the minds of your listeners."

Tim did just that. When he closed his final speech, even Mr. Rohmer appeared moved. The marks Tim received for both speeches more than made up for the points he had lost on the debate.

To Tim's surprise, Isaac echoed Ward's idea. "These speeches are too good for our small class," Isaac told him after school that afternoon. "Have you thought of sending them to the *Liberator*?"

"It could cause a great deal of grief for my family if they were published," Tim said.

"It could. And at the same time," Isaac retorted, "it could change the hearts and minds of many readers. I was watching the reactions in the classroom, and even Hollis was bug-eyed as he listened."

Isaac was right. The time had come for Tim to decide if he was truly ready to take a stand.

Walking home from school that afternoon, Pam was all excited. "Tim, you'll never guess who's coming to Cincinnati to visit. I found out from Sybil just today."

Tim barely had time to answer "Who?" before she blurted out the answer.

"Why Malvina Dorchester! Of all people. Isn't that glorious news? She's coming for an extended summer visit. I'm so excited. She may be here by my birthday."

Tim remembered his conversation with Malvina and her knowledge of Cincinnati politics. Why would she be coming to their city of all places?

"Well, aren't you the least bit excited?" Pam looked at him, then shook her head. "I'm beginning to worry about you again. Too much study is making you unfeeling."

Tim smiled inwardly at the irony of her words. Unfeeling. Sometimes his feelings ripped through him with such force, it was as though his gut were being wrenched out.

"You'll be kind to her, won't you?" Pam asked.

"Perhaps I won't have the opportunity."

"But, Tim, you must take the opportunity. The Scriptures clearly tell us in Romans 12 that we are to be 'given to hospitality.' I believe the Lord wants us to be kind to all. 'Be kindly affectioned one to another with brotherly love,' " she quoted as she swung her folded parasol. "I believe you're too hard on folks, Tim. You show justice, but there is no room for mercy."

Tim was amazed at how little his sister truly understood. Didn't the slaves qualify for brotherly love? But he held his peace. He couldn't convince her. Pam's mind was made up.

"I suppose the evening of my birthday party, you'll be stuffed in your room and won't even make an appearance. Your own sister. How can you be so unkind to those you love the most?"

Ward had taught Tim much about not reacting to people's words. "Look deeper," he had instructed. "Listen for meaning."

"I'll be at your birthday party, Pam," Tim assured her. "I wouldn't miss it. Why, I'll even dance a quadrille with you."

Just those few words put a smile on her face.

The pressures of studies had slacked off, which gave Tim time to meticulously copy his speeches. When finished, he mailed them to the *Liberator*. He decided that mailing would be better than dropping them off at the newspaper printing office.

Papa had asked that Tim begin working Saturdays at the boatworks, and Tim agreed. "For the present, I'll have you work with our bookkeeper," Papa said, "and he can teach you the books and accounts."

Never had time dragged by so slowly as it did when Tim was working on the ledger books in the office of the Lankford and Allerton Boatworks. He sensed none of the challenge that he had with his studies, or with his speeches, or with Ward's law books. And this was only on Saturdays. By summer, he would be at the boatworks each and every day.

In the back of his mind, he kept thinking that if he agreed

to work with Papa, perhaps in a year or so Papa would give him permission to study at Harvard. He held onto that hope.

Mama hired extra help to prepare the house for Pam's party. Extra cooks assisted Willa, and workers were brought in to serve. During the afternoon preceding the party, the house swarmed with people involved in the preparations.

There was to be a formal dinner followed by dancing. Mama directed the workers to move the drawing room furniture against the walls so that the room could accommodate a small orchestra and there would be space for a dance floor. While the house was nothing compared to Beckworth Manor, the preparations seemed to please Pam.

The warm May weather allowed all the windows to be flung open wide and the house to be aired out. There wasn't a corner in the house that hadn't been scrubbed spotless.

Tim had been duly warned by all family members to act like a gentleman. "And remember," Mama added, "these are guests in our home. I'll thank you to leave your political thinking to another time and place."

Tim promised he would. When Malvina arrived along with the O'Bannon family, Tim remained polite, yet cool. Seeing Hollis Bodley arrive with his parents nearly knocked Tim off his feet. No one had given him an inkling that this was planned. But what could he do? Again, he was forced to shake hands, greet, be sociable, and dutifully bite his tongue.

Pam had been instructed by those "in the know" not to make her appearance until all the guests had arrived. She then walked elegantly down the front stairway while everyone below hollered out "Hip hip hurrah!" and "Happy Birthday!" Tim himself had to admit his sister was quite a lovely young lady.

Dinner went off without a hitch, and Tim was pleased that his sister seemed to be having the time of her life. Thankfully, Mama and Pamela had arranged for Malvina to be seated several spaces away from him. Hollis, too, was far away from where Tim sat.

True to his promise, Tim danced with Pamela, but only for two dances. From then on, she had no other dances free. She was definitely the belle of her own ball.

Later, during a break in the festivities, several of the young people were standing about the refreshment tables. Sitting nearby on a settee pushed against the wall, Tim was paying scant attention when he heard his name mentioned.

"Pamela Allerton," Malvina was saying. "You never told me that your brother was an author."

"Tim? Why he's no author," Pam answered with a giggle.

Tim looked over their way, and Malvina caught his eyes. "Why, Pam dear, you are just too, too modest." The lovely dark-eyed girl reached into the pocket of her crimson silk skirt and pulled out what appeared to be a newspaper clipping.

Tim felt himself tense.

"Just looky here what I found in the *Liberator* this very day," she said in her honey drawl. Ceremoniously she unfolded the piece and held it up. "It says right here, 'At the Cabin Door, an essay by Timothy Allerton.' " She turned her dark eyes to Tim once again. "Now that is you, isn't it, Timothy Allerton?"

Pam gasped. "Oh, Tim, no!"

Hollis gallantly stepped to Pam's side and took her arm to steady her. "It's exactly what I've been telling you, Pamela. Your brother may seem quiet, but he plans things in a devious way to get the most attention. He cannot be trusted."

With that, Pam gave a deep groan and fled from the room.

CHAPTER 14

Night Visitors

Things around the Allerton house were cool for a number of days following the party. Tim received a stern lecture from Papa, warning him once again that his views could harm the entire family. Of course Tim never dreamed that the article would appear the very day of Pam's party. But more than that, he never dreamed someone like Malvina would read the *Liberator*.

The awards Tim received at the school commencement exercises mattered little in the light of the problems at home. His family barely acknowledged his accomplishments.

Isaac was quick to say, "See, Tim? It's like I always said,

it never pays to try to please parents." But Tim hadn't studied hard to receive school awards, or to please his parents, but for his future at Harvard.

Mr. Rohmer had, in private, commended Tim on the published article. "I know this didn't happen without exacting a price," the kindly old instructor said.

Thinking of his deep humiliation at Pam's party, Tim had to agree. Yet compared to what others were doing, it was a small price to pay.

By June, Ward had gathered a strong core of black leaders who were presenting options and reasonable solutions to city hall to protect Little Africa. As summer heated up, so did the tempers of all those in city politics.

Busy at the boatworks each day, Tim rarely saw Pam except at supper, and even then she wouldn't look at him and seldom if ever spoke to him. She spent most days with Sybil and Malvina, as they scurried about town from one social function to the next.

As far as he knew, none of his family had actually read his article. And most likely they never would.

One evening Mama and Papa called Tim and Pam into the library to talk. This was odd. Tim couldn't imagine what occasion had called for a closed family meeting, which meant away from the ears of Uncle Ben and Willa.

The meeting was merely to discuss a trip to the country. "Betsy and Andrew have invited the two of you to come to the farm for a summer visit," Mama was saying.

Tim's first thought was that Papa couldn't spare him from the boatworks. His second thought was that Pam would never agree to go with him. He was wrong on both counts.

"With things in such uproar here in the city," Papa said, "we felt it would be a good thing for the two of you to accept the invitation." Looking at Tim, he added, "You may drive the smaller carriage."

"We felt you could leave by the end of the week," Mama said. "The country air will do both of you good. And Betsy seems to have her heart set on seeing you."

Tim wondered later if Pam had been ordered by Papa to go. She was still quiet as they drove out of the city that clear June morning. Papa insisted they leave at dawn so they would arrive before nightfall.

Tim couldn't remember a more uncomfortable time with his sister. Until they stopped at a wayhouse for their noon meal, she hardly said a word. The morning had been cool, and the black canvas carriage top had been folded down. But now that the sun would be overhead, Tim took the time to put the top up to keep his sister in the shade.

When they were underway once more, Pam thanked him for seeing to the carriage top. Then she said, "I suppose I shouldn't continue to be out of sorts with you since we're going to be among company. After all, Malvina says I should continue to be tolerant of you in spite of your radical views."

Tim held the reins steady, not wanting his father's feisty matched bays to take their head. "What else does Malvina Dorchester say?" he asked warily.

"Of course she's very tender and understanding. She says you have a good heart, but that you've just been misinformed." Then before he could answer, she went on. "Blacks are a lot like children, Tim. Malvina helped me see that if the planters didn't take care of them, they'd never be able to do so on their own."

Tim wanted to point out to her that educated Ward Baker seemed to be doing quite well on his own, but he held his tongue. He could learn more by simply letting her talk.

"They're like children, she says?"

Pam nodded. "But she says she could never expect you to understand since you've never lived right among them."

"And she lives right among them?"

"Oh, of course. Many of their slaves are right there in the house."

Tim could hardly believe this distortion of the truth. "Well, I'm just thankful that you've decided to be tolerant of my views," he said, bringing the subject back around.

"As tolerant as one can be under the circumstances," she answered coolly.

No matter what the reason was that they'd come to the farm, Tim found himself extremely grateful. The down-to-earth Farley family presented a refreshing contrast to the pomp and arrogance of Beckworth Manor and Pam's new friends. Tim watched as even Pam seemed to forget her city manners and relaxed with the Farley children.

Tim wore some of Andrew's plain work clothes and helped to cut the hay in the meadow. He enjoyed the feel of the sun beating down on his back and the sweat pouring off his face. He breathed in the sweet aroma of new-mown hay and laughed as he scared up cottontail bunnies and coveys of bobwhite. When blisters surfaced on Tim's hands, Andrew teased him about being like a cultured hothouse flower. The good-natured teasing of Andrew was gentle and easy to take.

Tim had brought along a couple law books, but there was precious little time to open them. The Farleys worked from sunup until sundown with barely time to rest, especially now that summer harvest was upon them.

One evening, Tim was awakened by voices downstairs. He'd been given a bed in five-year-old Calvin's room at the far end of the upstairs hall. Wondering what was happening, he went down to see. He found Betsy in the kitchen and asked if she needed his help.

Betsy waved him on back to bed. "It's nothing but a sick calf," she said. "Happens all the time." She was lifting a lidded kettle off the stove.

"For the calf?" he asked, pointing to the kettle.

She nodded. "Mm hm. Special formula."

"I can help carry."

She shook her head. "We farm women are used to it."

Tim let it go and went back upstairs. But he didn't return to his bed. Instead he peeked in the master bedroom and saw that Andrew was also gone. Pulling on his boots and trousers, he slipped out the back door and made his way quietly to the barn. In the shadows, he came up under one of the windows and crouched down. He had no thought of going in. He merely wanted to listen.

Soon he heard the buzzing of soft voices and a few clinks of metal against metal, like forks on tin plates. No voice was distinct, but he determined there were at least two other people beside Betsy and Andrew. He was fairly certain that his favorite cousins were hiding slaves in their barn.

Before returning to the house, he stood up to take one quick look in the barn window. There he saw Andrew pushing back hay and opening a hidden trapdoor in the floor. Down into the opening went a black man and a young black woman with a babe in her arms. Happy and satisfied, Tim returned quickly to the house and his bed. He couldn't remember ever feeling so exhilarated. It was as though everything he'd tried to stand for in the past months had suddenly been confirmed.

The next morning Tim was awake almost before the noisy rooster set up his crowing on the back fence. Being careful not to awaken young Calvin, he dressed and hurried downstairs. Betsy stood in the kitchen at the stove frying potatoes. The aroma was heavenly.

Coming up behind her, Tim said softly, "I want you to know I'm pleased that you and Andrew are caring for sick calves."

She looked at him and smiled. "We're pleased to do it."

"How I wish I could do the same."

Betsy put down her spoon and put her arm about his shoulders. "Didn't I hear about some cattle thieves in Cincinnati trying to make off with a sick calf? And didn't those thieves wind up in the icy river water and the calf get rescued?"

Tim laughed outright. "How did you know about that?"

"Word spreads quickly among those who are in the business." Turning back to her work, she added, "Something tells me, Timothy, that one day you'll be helping more sick calves than all the rest of us put together."

"I hope so, Betsy. I truly hope so." He wanted to ask a million questions, but Pam and the Farley children were coming down the stairs for breakfast. It was time for him to eat and get out in the meadow to help Andrew.

A few days later, a man on horseback came riding up to the house to talk to Andrew. It was a neighbor whose heifer was having a bad time calving. "It's an awful thing to ask at haying time," the neighbor said, "but I don't want to lose this calf. Could you come and help?"

Andrew looked at Tim. "Could you look after things here? I'll be back tomorrow morning as early as possible."

Tim nodded, wondering if this calving was similar to the "sick calf" of a few day earlier. He assured Andrew he'd keep the scythe going in the hay meadow till he got back.

"Thanks, Tim."

117

After Andrew rode off, Tim felt the sudden weight of responsibility. It was a little frightening. Of course he wasn't able to cut nearly as much hay as Andrew, but he kept a good pace until dusk. After supper he tumbled into bed with weariness.

He wasn't sure if he'd been asleep when he felt a touch on his arm. He opened his eyes to see Betsy's tall form bending over him. She put her fingers to her lips. Softly she said, "Get dressed. I need your help."

"Sick calves?"

She nodded and then was gone. In a flash, Tim was dressed and downstairs to the kitchen. There again was the big lidded kettle along with a large basket full of bread, cheese, fruit, and boiled eggs.

"A large group," she said, handing him the basket.

Without speaking he followed her to the barn. There in the back, in the shadows of the grain bin, were seven black folk huddled together. Lines of fatigue were etched deeply into their faces.

Betsy showed Tim where the tin plates and cups were hidden. He helped her quickly pass out food to every person. Betsy opened the door to the large grain bin and allowed them to go inside to sit down and eat their food.

"Here, Tim," Betsy said. "You hold the child while they eat."

She handed him a tiny baby wrapped in a ragged dirty shawl. "I'm going back in the house to get a fresh blanket and milk for her." She paused. "Her name is DeEtta."

"Which one's the mother?" he whispered.

"Shot," Betsy answered softly.

The word was like ice water in Tim's face. "Slave catchers?"

Betsy nodded. "She was only sixteen."

118

Tim took DeEtta, sat down in the hay, and leaned back against a feed bunk. In a few minutes, he heard the door open again and expected to see Betsy. To his surprise, it was Pamela. "Tim, are you here?" she called out. "Is everything all right?"

She stopped, staring in shock at Tim sitting there with a baby nestled in his arms. "Tim? What are you doing? Is that a baby?"

CHAPTER 15

Saving the Baby

Tim said nothing as Pamela drew her long ruffled shawl more tightly about her dressing gown. It never occurred to him that she might come out to the barn in the dark all by herself.

"I heard noises," she said, "and thought something was amiss."

Just then, Betsy came in behind Pam. "Nothing is amiss, Pamela. Everything's fine. Have you ever changed a pair of nappies?"

"Me? Why no."

"Well, now that you're out here, make yourself useful and put these on the infant." Betsy held out the folded cloth to Pam, but Pam just looked at her.

"Go on now. We haven't much time."

Pam took hesitant steps toward Tim. Tim lay DeEtta in the hay and unwrapped the ragged cloth that had served as her blanket. Pam knelt down, and the tiny baby looked up at her with wide dark eyes and cooed and gurgled.

"Tim? Is this a child of a runaway slave?" she whispered.

Tim nodded. "Her name is DeEtta." He motioned to the grain bin. "Seven are hiding in there."

With a bit of struggle, Pam was able to get the nappies on the infant. Taking the clean blanket given her by Betsy, she proceeded to wrap the small body carefully in the blanket, then lifted the child in her arms. Tim watched as a tiny brown fist closed around Pam's forefinger.

Betsy brought a bowl and a piece of cloth. "We're going to try to get a little milk down her by dropping it from the cloth," Betsy explained.

"But what about the mother?" Pam asked.

"The mother's dead, Pam," Tim told her.

Pam's eyes grew large as she slowly grasped the meaning of his words. "Was she killed by. . ." She couldn't finish her sentence.

"Shot to death by slave catchers. She was only sixteen."

"Why did they shoot her?"

"They don't need a reason," Betsy answered.

Pam squeezed her eyes shut as though to close out the raw ugly truth. "Give me the bowl," she said.

Together they tried to feed the tiny infant goat's milk.

"What will happen to her after they leave?"

Tim shook his head. "That's not up to us. We can only do what we can here."

"But she may die. Oh, Tim, we can't let her die." Pam touched the baby's soft velvety cheek, then looked at him.

By the distraught look on her face, Tim knew that at last his sister understood his feelings.

Just then, Tim thought of the couple with the baby who had stopped over two nights earlier.

"Betsy," he said. "What if I were able to take this infant to the mother who came through the other night? Couldn't she be a wet nurse and perhaps save DeEtta's life?"

Betsy shook her head. "I don't know, Tim. There're slave catchers out there everywhere just waiting for us to make a wrong move in a desperate situation. The father may not want to separate from her."

"We could hide the father beneath hay in the buckboard."

"And I could carry the child," Pam spoke up.

"You?" Tim was incredulous.

"It would appear perfectly natural for the two of us to be riding along and me holding a child."

"She's right," Betsy said. "I'll ask the father."

Betsy left them to discuss the proposal with the leader and the baby's father. A tall serious black man, not unlike Ward, came to where Pam was holding the child. Betsy introduced him as Mr. Elihu, the leader and guide. "Mr. Elihu is a teacher in Canada and comes through two or three times a year with a new group."

Pam shook her head. "You're free, yet you come back to help others?" Tim could tell she was having difficulty grasping the truth.

Mr. Elihu didn't acknowledge her question. "Jewett, the child's father, understands there's risk," he said to Betsy, "but he's willing to take that risk for the sake of the infant and in honor of the mother. If they hadn't escaped, the child and mother would have been sold away from him. No risk is too great now."

122

BOOK 16—ESCAPE FROM SLAVERY

It was settled. While Pamela changed into one of Betsy's calico day dresses, Tim hitched the team to the buckboard and they filled it with hay. The other fugitives would be taken through the tunnel beneath the barn to the cave by the creek bank. There they would hide until the next evening and slip away in the dark.

Betsy drew a map for Tim. "Mr Elihu suggests you bypass the first stop from here and continue on to the second. This creates a better chance of overtaking the nursing mother." Handing Tim the map, she said, "When you knock on the front door, say you have a message from Mr. Elihu. They'll invite you inside. Refuse their offer, and ask to take the horses to the barn."

Tim listened carefully to the instructions. His heart pounded in his ears.

Betsy suggested to Pam that she use a wet comb on her fashionable sausage curls and smooth them straight back, fastening her hair in a knot in back. Then she gave Pam a cotton sunbonnet to wear.

As dawn was barely touching the horizon with a pink tinge, they were ready to go. Tim helped Pam up into the buckboard, after which Betsy handed up the swaddled infant. Jewett, the baby's father, was buried in loose hay in the back. Betsy provided him with a clean cloth to keep his mouth and nose protected from the hay dust. She also loaded two baskets of food to make their cargo look even more typical for a buckboard on a country road.

"The ride takes just over an hour," Betsy explained, "so I'll expect you back here before noon."

Tim nodded and gave the reins a shake. The strong team of plow horses stepped out easily.

The farm roads were unmercifully bumpy, and Tim knew

Jewett's ride in the back must be extremely uncomfortable. The curving road wound in and out of thick stands of trees, then broke into open fields of rye, wheat, and barley, all nearly ready for cutting.

"You look right nice in calico and a sunbonnet," Tim said, making an effort at humor. Pam had said little since they started.

Now she looked over at him. "When we return to Cincinnati," she said in a serious tone, "may I read your article that was published?"

Tim smiled. "Sooner than that. I happen to have it with me at Betsy's house."

When they were about halfway there, the baby began to fuss. Pam was a novice at handling babies, and Tim could tell she was nervous about how to handle the infant.

"What'll I do, Tim?"

"What about the sugar bag?"

"Oh, yes." Reaching into the basket at her feet, she rummaged about for the tiny bag that Betsy had made.

"The baby may suck on this," Betsy had told them. "It's not much, but it'll have to do till you get there."

For a time, DeEtta did suck on the sugar bag, but before long, her tummy told her she wasn't getting any food. Her fussing turned to loud cries.

"Just a ways longer." Tim studied the map again, then returned it to his pocket. As he did, he looked up and saw two men riding hard and fast toward them through a hay field to the east. "Uh oh," he said.

Pam saw them and gasped. She tucked the blankets more tightly around the infant, put her up over her shoulder, and patted her back in an attempt to calm her. But the hungry infant cried all the more.

"Ho, there," one of the riders yelled as they approached. Tim could tell in an instant they were slave catchers. They wore the filth of long hours in the saddle. "Morning," Tim said, as the men drew to a stop. Reluctantly, he pulled on the reins. DeEtta continued to set up her hungry wail.

The men studied them with hardened stares. One was older with a thick black beard. The other was somewhat younger with wispy sideburns.

"You younguns seen a bunch of black folk along the way? We're on the trail of a large passel of 'em," said the bearded one.

Tim shook his head. "Do runaway slaves take to the main roads these days?"

The men looked at one another. "That your kid?" the younger one asked Pam. Pam nodded, and Tim was thankful the sunbonnet covered her fear-filled eyes.

"Well, why can't you make it stop that infernal squalling?" the older one demanded.

The younger one rode around to Pam's side of the buckboard.

"Let's see that noisy kid," he said.

Pam looked over at him. "You have children?" she asked.

He shook his head. "Not me. I gots a heap of nieces and nephews, though."

"Then perhaps you've seen measles. Could you come close and look here and tell me if these spots are measles?" She rested the tiny bundle on her lap and acted as though she were going to take off the blanket. Tim felt his breath catch in his throat.

"Naw," said the young man pulling back on the reins of his horse. "Naw, I don't know nothing 'bout no measles. 'Cept that they spread like a brushfire in August." He looked over at the other man. "Come on, Uncle Wally. We just wasting time here. We got slaves to catch."

Pam reached into the basket at her feet and pulled out two apples. "Here," she said, tossing an apple to each man. "I'm sure you're hungry."

"Thank you kindly, ma'am," said the uncle, reaching out to catch the fruit. With that, they turned and rode off.

"Good day, gentlemen," Tim called after them as he shook the reins.

Tim and Pam rode a ways without speaking. Pam patted and cooed to the baby in an attempt to comfort her.

At last Tim said, "I think that must be it." He pointed toward a small farm in a shallow valley. The landmarks agreed with Betsy's map.

Tim pulled up in the front dooryard. A lady dressed in homespun came out on the front porch. When Tim said he had a message from Mr. Elihu, the lady invited them to come in. But Tim asked if he could take the horses to the barn first, and she said yes.

Once the wagon was inside the barn and the door was closed, Tim and Pam helped Jewett out of the hay. He took the squalling baby from Pam's arms with his profound thanks.

The lady, whose name was Martha, informed them that the mother with the infant was hiding up in their hayloft that very moment. The couple and child had arrived in the night. Tim felt almost faint with relief.

Holding his infant daughter, Jewett grabbed the ladder with one hand and pulled himself up into the loft. They heard the mother softly talking to her new "adopted" child, and within moments, the sounds of pitiful wailing were silenced.

"No need of us staying out here," Martha said, opening

the large double doors of the barn. "Won't you come in for a bite to eat?"

Tim shook his head. "We must get back. But we brought provisions." As he unloaded the baskets onto her front porch, he told her of the large group that was close on the heels of the couple she was already hiding.

She nodded and smiled as though it were nothing out of the ordinary. "We'll be ready."

"We came across slave catchers on the road," Pam told her.

"I'm not surprised. They spend a lot of time combing all over Ohio. They mostly come up empty handed."

Tim told Martha of Pam's question about measles and how it made them decide to look elsewhere. Martha laughed and complimented Pam on her quick thinking.

"We've all learned to think quick to stay ahead of those butchers," she said. Then she sighed and pushed strands of hair into her loose bun. "I wonder though how much longer the South can hold onto those whose hearts yearn for freedom. Freedom at any price."

Back at the Farleys' home, Pam read Tim's article. "You're such an apt writer," she said when she finished reading it. "Every point is crystal clear."

"Only to those who want to hear," Tim countered.

"Yes," she agreed, "to those who want to hear."

The time for them to load up and return to Cincinnati came much too soon for Tim. Helping the Farleys with the farming was satisfying, but helping with the runaway slaves was nothing short of exhilarating. He couldn't wait to tell Isaac all about it. But not even assisting runaway slaves could match his joy at having gained his sister's sympathy and understanding.

Calvin and Rachel hated to see their guests leaving. In manly fashion, Calvin shook hands with Tim, but Rachel gave hugs to both of them. Betsy and Andrew complimented Tim and Pam on being such a help.

"I'm not sure what would have happened if you'd not been here," Betsy told them. "The baby might not have made it."

Pam, once again dressed in her silk dress and flowered straw bonnet, said, "I'm thankful to God for allowing me to help."

And Tim could tell she meant every word.

As they talked along the way home, they both decided they would tell their parents nothing of what had taken place. Tim was still unsure of his father's views on the issues of slavery and the black laws.

"The slaves I saw in Mississippi, those who appeared to be so happy," Pam said, "they weren't really happy, were they?"

"Would you be?" Tim asked.

Pam thought for a moment as though the truth were slowly being revealed. "No matter how they are treated, they're still slaves, aren't they? And they long to be free!"

Tim nodded. "That's right. And that's why they are escaping by the scores, right from under the noses of their owners."

Tim and Pam returned to a warm welcome from their parents. For supper that evening, Willa prepared berry pies from the fruit that Tim and Pam had brought from the farm, along with baked squash and roasting ears.

Conversation centered around the farm and all that was happening there. Mama commented on how brown Tim had become. Neither his parents nor Uncle Ben said a word about all the uproar that was happening in the city, but Tim found out rather quickly.

After supper, he saddled Fearnaught and headed straight for Ward's house. As Ward had asked those long weeks ago, Tim rode into Little Africa the back way and hid his horse behind the Bakers' frame house.

Clara's tummy was quite large now beneath her muslin dress. The baby would arrive in about a month. Tim was disturbed to see her face tired and drawn and her eyes with dark circles beneath them.

"Tim," she said as she let him inside, "you shouldn't come here anymore. It's too dangerous. It could cause trouble for your family and for us as well."

Tim didn't know what to say, but Ward quickly appeared and put his arm about his wife's shoulders. "It's all right, Clara," he said to her in a gentle tone. "Tim's our friend."

"It doesn't matter," she said, shaking her head. Unchecked tears spilled onto her ebony cheeks. "They don't care."

"Please prepare something for our guest," Ward told her, then he motioned for Tim to join him in his office. Once the door was closed, Ward showed Tim a copy of the *Daily Gazette*.

A harsh article called for a demand to be given to the blacks living in Cincinnati. They should have to obey the black laws. "We must," the article read, "remove that population from our territory while the power is still in our hands."

Tim looked up at Ward. "To drive free citizens from their homes—how can that be any worse than slavery?"

CHAPTER 16
The Plot

After Tim and Pam had been home a couple weeks, Mama commented that Pam didn't "seem herself these days." Mama was sure her daughter was coming down with something and gave her a spoonful of terrible-tasting dark-colored tonic every evening before bedtime. Tim knew Pam wasn't sick. He knew exactly what was bothering his sister.

Late in July, the Society of St. Cecilia was due to meet at the Allerton home. Pamela, Mama, and Willa spent hours preparing the house for their distinguished young guests. They were scheduled to have a teatime and sewing circle. Everything was in order, but Tim could tell that Pam's usual exuberance was missing.

That evening, following the social event, Tim went to the stables to groom Fearnaught. Pam came out to join him. Tim had made it a point to stay away from all the goings on, choosing to take supper in the kitchen and then make a quick exit. Papa was still at the boatworks working late.

"You brush that horse anymore, and I dare say all his hair will be gone," she said as she came around and sat down on a tack box.

"He looks wonderful, doesn't he?" Tim stepped back to admire the glossy coat of the roan. "I don't believe I've ever seen him so fit." Tim knew Pam hadn't come out to admire his horse. "How was the society meeting?"

"It went well. Sybil told me it was the best she'd ever attended."

Tim nodded and went back to brushing and currying Fearnaught's coat.

"Malvina came."

"I suspected as much. She's attended just about everything there is to attend in Cincinnati since she arrived."

Pam ignored his remark. "She engaged me in a rather odd conversation."

Tim looked at her. "About slavery?"

"Oh, no, she'd never talk to me about that. It was about us."

"You and I?"

Pam nodded. "And our trip to the Farleys' farm."

Tim stopped brushing and came over to where she was sitting. "Tell me more."

"She wanted to know where we went and what we did. Although she made it seem like light conversation, I felt like I was being interrogated."

She wrinkled her freckled nose, always more covered with freckles in the summer. "Is it because I now have something to hide that I feel this way?"

Tim went back to brushing to hide how concerned he was. He'd always felt uncomfortable around Malvina

131

Dorchester, and he had never trusted her. Malvina's knowledge of the politics in Cincinnati wasn't normal for a young lady her age who lived in a different state.

"What did you tell her?"

"At first, I tried to avoid her questions, but it became rather awkward. Then Sybil walked up and filled in the answers, explaining that we had relatives who live on a farm in the country."

Just why Malvina would be snooping, Tim wasn't sure, but it was obvious to him that she wasn't in the city on a social holiday.

"I feel differently toward Malvina now, Tim," Pam continued. "I thought I was being kind and hospitable toward her. But I just wanted to be nice so she would like me. I was impressed by her clothes and her genteel manner."

Tim wanted to order Pam to stay away from the girl, but Pam would have to decide that for herself. "What do you plan to do?" he asked.

She shrugged. "I don't know what to do. Sybil and all the other girls hold Malvina in high esteem just as I did before . . . well, before my experience at the Farleys'. It would hurt terribly to be left out of all the activities."

She paused. "I plan to pray and ask God for wisdom, then try to walk where He leads me."

"That's a great plan." Tim put down the brush, unhooked the cross-ties, and led Fearnaught back to his stall. "I'm proud of you, Pam," he said.

"Thank you," she said quietly.

The office at the boatworks where Tim worked was stuffy and hot. Each day he sat in front of massive account books, meticulously logging figures and drafting invoices and bills of lading. But the next day, it was almost unbearable. The numbers seemed to swim before his eyes.

August was half over, and the temperature was up in the nineties. He kept getting up and going to the water pitcher for another cup of water. By late afternoon, he finally realized he must be coming down with something. And here Pam was the one who'd been taking all the tonic.

That night, Tim and Isaac planned to attend another city council meeting, so he told no one how terrible he felt. Together they had attended two previous meetings, watching as Ward Baker and his hand-picked men presented their petitions for leniency. The meetings both angered and frightened Tim. Though the arguments were clear and well presented, the black men were usually shouted down. It was as if no one wanted to hear their views.

Tim hadn't seen Ward for several days. It wasn't safe for any white person to be seen in Little Africa. The tension was too high.

At supper Tim made an attempt to eat. Mama quickly noticed that his appetite was less than usual.

"It's just the heat," Tim told her.

"I believe it's all that worrying you do," Mama answered. "I'll swan, you worry and wool things about in that head of yours more than ten people could do. I wish you'd stay out of all the mess that's going on in town. That's what's making you feel poorly."

Tim tried to straighten up and eat another helping of mutton chops.

"Are you going to the town meeting tonight?" Papa asked.

Tim nodded. "But I'll come home early, I promise. And I'll go straight to bed."

"See that you do," Mama said sternly.

That was close. If Mama had laid her hand upon his hot forehead, he'd have been in bed that instant. Tim quickly saddled Fearnaught and rode to Isaac's house. Together they rode to the lyceum, where the city meetings were held. The building was packed.

The joker that Isaac used to be had disappeared over the past few months. Blue eyes that once sparkled with mischief now burned with passion. Tim followed as Isaac pressed through the crowd. Though there were no more seats, Isaac moved to a side wall near the front, where they could stand and still watch.

Of all the meetings they had attended, this was by far the worst. It was obvious that city councilors were ready to take action. If they didn't use the law, they were ready to use mobs. Tim's head spun as voices shouted and the suffocating closeness pressed in on him.

His heart grieved as he saw Ward repeatedly attempt to have his say. No one listened. By the time the meeting was adjourned, Tim was near to collapse.

It was then that Isaac noticed Tim's condition. "Timothy, you look like a ghost. Are you gonna pass out on me?"

No words would come out. Tim vaguely remembered Isaac hanging on to him and scooting him out a side exit, then helping him up on Fearnaught. "I'll ride to your house with you," he said.

Mama fed Tim the nasty-tasting tonic and put him straight to bed. Through the night, she placed cool cloths on his face and chest to bring the fever down.

He lay there, barely able to move all through the long night and the next day. Nightmares of Ward and Clara raged through his mind. He needed to get up and help them. He must get up. But his body refused to move.

"Tim. Tim." A voice floated through the air to his brain. "It's me, Pam. Can you hear me?"

"What time is it?" he asked. He forced his eyes open to see darkness outside the windows. He looked at Pam. She was wearing her riding cloak. He pushed to lift himself up on his elbow.

"It's nearly eleven." She knelt down by his bed. "Tim, I've just seen Malvina riding past in her carriage. She was all alone. I've saddled Fearnaught. I'm going to follow her."

Tim pushed now to sit up. "I'll go."

"No. Lie still. I'll report what I find." She rose and turned to go. "Pray for me."

He heard her steps going quietly down the back stairs. He forced himself to get up and go to the window. He watched as his sister rode off toward town on his horse.

It was all he could do to get himself back into bed. Crazy Pam. His tolerant and merciful sister. How she'd changed. "God," he prayed under his breath, "I'm partly to blame for her change of heart. Now I ask that you protect her from harm."

He had no idea how much time passed before Pam was once again in his room. Her eyes were wide.

"What is it?" he wanted to know.

"She's spying."

"Malvina?"

Pam nodded.

"I thought as much. What kind of spying? For whom?"

"For a group of plantation owners. They want to know the key people in the city who are sympathetic to runaway slaves."

"Where did you hear all this?"

Pam helped him to push up pillows behind his head so he could sit up. "Malvina went to Bodley's Jewelers. I rode

135

down the alleyway to the back. The window to the office was open, and I heard her, Mr. Bodley, and several others talking. Oh, Tim," she said, her voice breaking. "They mentioned your friend Ward."

Now Tim sat up. "Ward? What did they say?"

"They called him a ring leader and a rabble-rouser. One of the men said, 'Getting him out of the area is imperative.' And Mr. Bodley answered, 'Or we'll get rid of him altogether.' "

Suddenly Tim was out of bed, pulling on his trousers, shirt, and boots. "We've got to get Ward out of there. You ride to get Isaac and have him meet me at the livery."

Leaning a little on Pam's arm, Tim made his way down the back stairway. At the bottom of the stairs stood Papa with his arms folded and a scowl on his face. "Where do you two think you're going?"

CHAPTER 17

Mob Violence

"Ward's in danger," Tim said, struggling to put strength into his voice. "I'm going to go get him and Clara out of Little Africa."

"It's dangerous out there," Papa said, "and you're sick."

"I don't care if it's dangerous, and I'm not sick anymore. Pam just heard men saying Ward is a ring leader, and they aim to get rid of him. Do you know what that means, Papa?" Tim was near to tears. "That means no matter what happens to anyone else in Little Africa, Ward is targeted."

"Where would you take him?"

Tim hadn't even thought that far. "To Andrew and Betsy, I suppose." He thought about Clara, who was due to have her baby at any moment.

137

Papa put his hand on Tim's shoulder. "Your uncle Ben and I will go with you, Son."

If there'd been time, and if he'd had the strength, Tim would have whooped with joy. But there wasn't a moment to lose.

While Pam went to fetch Isaac, Papa went to the livery to rent a covered wagon. Papa said it would look less conspicuous if he went alone. Uncle Ben and Tim were to wait for him at the corner of Fourth and Vine.

Within the hour, the three were in the wagon on their way to Ward's house. They pulled the wagon around to the back of the house. At first Ward was reluctant to load up and leave. "I have to stay and help my people," he said. "You take Clara and Joseph."

Tim and Uncle Ben were already carrying out armloads of books from Ward's office. Clara was begging Ward to come with them. "Don't leave me," she cried. "Please, Ward, come with us."

Finally, Papa put his hands on Ward's shoulders. "Mr. Baker," he said in a gentle tone. "I've heard many good things about you from my son. I realize now that you are well equipped to help many people. But you cannot help them if you are dead. Take your wife and child and come with us. If nothing happens here, you can always come back."

Never had Tim been so proud of his father. He watched in amazement as Ward blinked back tears. "Thank you, Mr. Allerton. Of course you're right." He began helping to carry out his most important papers and case files. Clara, unable to move very fast, grabbed pictures from off the walls.

Suddenly Isaac burst through the Bakers' back door with a look of panic in his eyes. "They're coming!" he said. "An angry mob! Get out as quick as you can!" He pointed toward town, and sure enough, the eerie light of pine torches could be seen in the distance.

There was no time to lose. "Let me drive, Papa," Tim said. "I know how to get out of here the back way."

Ward, Clara, and Joseph were helped into the back of the covered wagon with their belongings. Tim, Papa, and Ben were in front. Trying not to panic, they thought of ways to make their renting the wagon look as logical and ordinary as possible. In spite of the fact that most people's attention would be distracted by the actions of the mob, they couldn't be too careful.

They drove out of Little Africa through the back way, then drove down toward the river and around by the landing. Papa purposely had Tim stop at the boatworks, where Papa went into the office as though he were doing late-night business. After that, they drove on toward home as though they were in no big hurry. The wagon was taken inside the carriage house, and the big doors were closed.

Quietly, under cover of darkness, they spirited the little family from the carriage house into the Allerton home. By then the sky to the west was aglow. While no one spoke of it, they knew that the mob must be burning out the black community. Tim felt heartsick.

Mama, Pam, and Willa scurried about to put out food for the unexpected nighttime guests. After they'd been fed, Mama took the oil lamp and said, "We have an attic room where you'll be comfortable. Come, I'll show you."

As they turned to follow, Ward looked around at the Allertons and smiled. "I felt sure Timothy came from good stock, and I was right. May the Lord reward each of you richly for saving our lives," he said simply. Wide-eyed

Joseph silently clung to his father's neck.

When they were gone, Tim collapsed onto a kitchen chair. Pam came over and felt his forehead. "Your fever's broken. How do you feel?"

"Weak as a newborn colt."

She patted his shoulder gently. "Did Isaac go on home?"

"Isaac! Oh no! Papa, I forgot all about Isaac. I thought he would come right behind us." He jumped to his feet. "I've got to go help him!"

"Timothy," Papa said, "you can't go back into that place. You'll get killed. You don't even know if Isaac is still there."

"I know him, Papa. He stayed to help. I just know he did. Please help me find him."

Just as Tim was moving toward the door, pounding startled each of them. "Tim!" someone shouted. "Mr. Allerton! Somebody! Open up!"

"That's Isaac!" Tim rushed to open the door. There stood Isaac, his clothes torn and bloodied. Leaning heavily against him was a bleeding, groaning, weeping Hollis Bodley.

Behind him, Tim heard Pam and Willa gasp at the sight.

"We need your help, Tim, old friend," Isaac said.

Immediately Papa and Uncle Ben were beside him, taking Hollis from Isaac's arms and laying him out on the kitchen floor. His shoulder was bleeding.

"Get blankets," Papa said to Pam. "Hurry. Willa, bring a pan of water."

"No one told me," Hollis was saying in a pitiful tone. "No one told me it would be so ghastly. So bloody. So merciless."

"Shush," Papa told him. "Lie still."

But Hollis tried to lift his head. "Why didn't they tell me, Mr. Allerton? Mobs are ruthless. I thought they would just try to scare them. Father told me we were going to scare them. Why didn't someone tell me they would burn and kill?"

"Some things, Hollis," Papa said softly, "we just have to learn on our own."

Tim knew that his father was referring to himself as well, and it brought hot tears to Tim's eyes.

"Where were you?" Tim asked Isaac. "I thought you would follow us out."

"I stayed to help as much as I could." He shook his head. "But when the mob arrived, there wasn't much anyone could do."

"Isaac saved my life, Tim," Hollis said. Then he groaned as Papa washed his wound. "I would have been trampled by the mob if he hadn't dragged me out of there. Shoulda listened to you, Tim. You were right about those poor defenseless people over there. Poor, poor defenseless people," he repeated as he wept like a baby.

"The bullet went clean through," Papa told him. "You'll be fine."

"I'll never be fine again," Hollis blubbered.

Willa busied herself caring for Isaac, cleaning his cuts and scratches.

In the midst of everything, Mama came into the room, her eyes wide. "My stars, we have a busy house this evening." Smiling, she added, "Mr. and Mrs. Ward Baker would like me to tell you they are the proud parents of a healthy baby son."

Tim looked over at Pam and smiled.

CHAPTER 18

Saying Good-bye

After more than half of Little Africa had been destroyed, it wasn't difficult to talk Ward into taking his family to Canada. Tim and Isaac planned to drive them to the Farleys just as soon as Clara was up and about.

Tim and Ward were in the carriage house boxing up the books and other belongings of Ward's that they had been able to save. The Bakers' home had been burned to the ground.

"We'll ship these to you as soon as you're settled in Canada," Tim told him. "You just write and let us know."

"Here," Ward said, reaching into the box. "I want you to have this set of James Madison's speeches. While I never agreed with some of his ideas on slavery, still he was a brilliant man."

"Thank you," Tim said, taking the books and stroking them reverently. "I guess no two people ever totally agree, do they?"

Ward shook his head. "Our creative Lord made us all too different for that."

"I was so wrong about Papa," Tim said. "I held anger in my heart against him because he didn't agree with me. And yet he helped rescue you and Clara and then opened the house to you. I was so wrong."

"And now?"

"I apologized to him for my anger. Then he apologized to me for not listening to me. And we both shed a few tears."

"It's all right for men to do that sometimes," Ward said. "To cry, I mean."

"And he says now that he's seen my strong determination, he promises to think about allowing me to attend Harvard."

Ward smiled. "You are truly a blessed young man, Timothy."

"I know." Tim put a few more books into the crate. It was sad to think about Ward leaving. They'd had so many good times together. Ward had taught him so much about so many things. Not just about debates and speaking, not just about fear and courage, but about life itself.

"Do you think I'll ever see you again?" Tim said, blinking back hot tears.

"I have no doubt of it, my friend." Ward put his large hand on Tim's shoulder. "After all, we attorneys will do well to keep in close contact with one another."

Tim smiled through his tears. "We attorneys will have to do just that!"

Further Reading

Ball, Charles. *Charles Ball and American Slavery.* History Eyewitness Series, ed. Jane Shuter. Austin, Tex.: Raintree/Steck Vaughn, 1995.

Douglass, Frederick. *Escape from Slavery: The Boyhood of Frederick Douglass in His Own Words.* New York: Knopf, 1994.

Fritz, Jean. *The Great Little Madison.* New York: Putnam Juvenile, 1989.

Hakim, Joy. *Liberty for All?* A History of US Series, Book 5. New York: Oxford University Press Children's Books, 1994.

————. *The New Nation.* A History of US Series, Book 4. New York: Oxford University Press Children's Books, 1994.

Hamilton, Virginia. *Many Thousand Gone: African Americans from Slavery to Freedom.* New York: Knopf, 1995.

Katz, William Loren. *Breaking the Chains: African-American Slave Resistance.* New York: Aladdin Paperbacks, 1998.

Kroll, Steven. *Robert Fulton: From Submarine to Steamboat.* New York: Holiday House, 1999.

Index